THE CASE OF THE WAFFLING WARRANTS

A Gossip Cozy Mystery Book 1

ROSIE A. POINT

Join my no-spam newsletter and receive an exclusive offer. Details can be found at the back of this book.

Cover by Mariah Sinclair | TheCoverVault.com

 Created with Vellum

MEET THE CHARACTERS

Charlie Smith (Mission)—An ex-spy, Charlie lives and works in her grandmother's inn in Gossip, Texas, as a server, maid, and assistant. With her particular set of skills and spunky attitude, she's become Gossip's "fixer" thanks to her previous involvement in solving murder mysteries.

Georgina Franklin (Mission)—Charlie's super-spy grandmother who raised her. Georgina (or Gamma, as Charlie calls her) is the most decorated spy in the history of the

NSIB. She's retired, but still as smart and spry as ever.

Lauren Harris—The happy-go-lucky chef at the Gossip Inn. A master baker, she's always got delicious cupcakes prepared for the inn's lunches and dinners. She's jolly, with bright red hair she wears in pigtails.

Cocoa Puff—Georgina's chocolate brown cat. He's friendly as can be with people he trusts. Often sleeps on Charlie's bed and accompanies her around the inn, helping her dust the various trinkets and tables.

Sunlight—Charlie's newly adopted cat and co-sleuth. A ginger kitty with an adventurous spirit. He loves to get up to mischief in the inn and always has Charlie's back.

Jessie Belle-Blue—Jessie is Georgina's worst nightmare. As the owner of the local cattery and now, a guesthouse, she hates the fact that Georgina has opened a kitten foster center in direct competition. Will do whatever it takes to come out on top.

Detective Aaron Goode—The new tough detective in town. He's handsome, with dark hair, a strong jawline, and unflinching determination to get to the bottom of things. He doesn't appreciate interferences.

Tina Rogers—Owner of the Bread Factory, a bakery that made specialty breads in town, she's recently fallen ill of the law and needs some help from Gossip's fixer.

Josie Carlson—Lauren's sister, and owner of another local bakery that specializes in cakes, The Little Cake Shop. She's blustery, full of herself, and enjoys bossing people around.

Mandy Gilmore—The town gossip who recently returned to Gossip after a failed business venture. Staying at the inn. Has big opinions about everyone and everything.

Opal Lister—A guest at the Gossip Inn, her house is currently being fumigated. She despises Mandy Gilmore and the gossipers of the town, even though she's one herself.

Bridget Willows—Head of the Gossip Sewing Club, she's always willing to share tips and tricks with young men and women interested in taking up the hobby.

A QUICK NOTE

*This is a short summary of what's happened prior to the events of the Gossip Series for those who haven't read the Mission Inn-possible Series. This is meant to provide some context for new readers, but feel free to skip this page if you want to avoid **spoilers** and plan on reading the Mission Inn-possible Series in the future.*

Charlotte Mission, now Smith, originally came to hide out at the Gossip Inn to avoid attention from her rogue spy ex-husband, Kyle Turner. She had outed him to her agency, the

NSIB (National Security Investigative Bureau), and he was determined to make her pay.

Thankfully, with the help of her retired spy grandmother, Georgina, she managed to solve several murders in the small town, Gossip, Texas, prevent mayhem, maintain her cover by the skin of her teeth, and see her ex-husband detained.

Charlie's ready to retire and relax... or so she thinks.

"Come in, Big G, come in." I spoke under my breath so that the flesh-colored microphone seated against my throat picked up my voice. "What is your status?"

My grandmother, Georgina—pet name Gamma, code name Big G—was out on a special operation. Reconnaissance at the newest guesthouse in our town, Gossip. The reason? First, she was an ex-spy, as was I, and second, the woman who'd opened the guesthouse was her mortal enemy and in direct competition with my grandmother's establishment, the Gossip Inn.

Who was this enemy, this bringer of potential financial doom?

A middle-aged woman with a penchant for wearing pashminas and annoying anyone who looked her way.

Jessie Belle-Blue.

It was rumored that even thinking the woman's name summoned a murder of crows.

"I repeat, Big G, what is your status?"

"I'm en route to the nest," my grandmother replied in my earpiece.

I let out a relieved sigh and exited my bedroom, heading downstairs to help with the breakfast service.

In the nine months since I had retired as a spy, life in Gossip had been normal. In the Gossip sense of the term. I'd expected that my job as a server, maid, and assistant would bring the usual level of "cat herding" inherent when working at the inn. Whether that involved tracking down runaway cats, literally, or providing a guest with a moist towelette after a fainting spell—tempers ran high in Gossip.

What was the reason for the craziness? Shoot, it had to be something in the water.

I took the main stairs two at a time and found my friend, the inn's chef, paging through her recipe book in the lime green kitchen. Lauren Harris wore her red hair in a French braid today, apron stretched over her pregnant belly.

"Morning," I said, "how are you today?"

"Madder than a fat cat on a diet." She slapped her recipe book closed and turned to me.

Uh oh. Looks like it's time for more cat herding.

"What's wrong?"

"My supplier is out of flour and sugar. Can you believe that?" Lauren huffed, smoothing her hands over her belly while the clock on the wall ticked away. Breakfast was in two hours and Lauren loved baking cupcakes as part of the meal.

"Do you have enough supplies to make cupcakes for this morning?"

"Yes. But just for today," Lauren replied.

"The guests are going to love my new waffle cupcakes, and they'll be sore they can't get anymore after this batch is done. Why, I should go down there and wring Billy's neck for doing this to me. He knows I take an order of sugar and flour every week, and I get it at just above cost too. What's Georgina going to say?"

"Don't stress, Lauren," I said. "We'll figure it out."

"Right." She brightened a little. "I nearly forgot you're the one who "fixes" things around here." Lauren winked at me.

She was the only person in the entire town who knew that my grandmother and I had once been spies for the NSIB—the National Security Investigative Bureau. But the news that I had helped solve several murders had spread through town, and now, anybody and everybody with a problem would call me up asking for help. A lot of them offered me money. And I was selective about who I chose to help.

"I'll check it out for you if you'd like," I said. "The flour issue."

"Nah, that's OK. I'm sure Billy will get more stock this week. I'll lean on him until he squeals."

"Sounds like you've been picking up tips from Georgina."

Lauren giggled then returned to her super-secret recipe book—no one but she was allowed to touch it.

"What's on the menu this morning?" I asked.

Lauren was the boss in the kitchen—she told me what to do, and I followed her instructions precisely. If I did anything else, like trying to read the recipe for instance, the food would end up burned, missing ingredients or worse.

The only place I wasn't a "fixer" was in the Gossip Inn's kitchen.

"Bacon and eggs over easy, biscuits and gravy, waffle cupcakes and... oh, I can't make fresh baked bread, can I?"

"Tell her I'll bring some back with me from the bakery." Gamma's voice startled me. Goodness, I'd forgotten about the earpiece— she could hear everything happening in the kitchen.

"I'll text Georgina and ask her to bring bread from the bakery."

"You're a lifesaver, Charlotte."

We set to work on the breakfast—it was 7:00 a.m. and we needed everything done within two hours—and fell into our easy rhythm of baking and cooking.

My grandmother entered the kitchen at around 8:30 a.m., dressed in a neat silk blouse and a pair of slacks rather than the black outfit she'd left in for her spy mission. Tall, willowy, and with neatly styled gray hair, Gamma had always reminded me of Helen Mirren playing the Queen.

"Good morning, ladies," she said, in her prim, British accent. "I bring bread and tidings."

"What did you find out?" I asked.

"No evidence of the supposed ghost tours," Gamma said.

We'd started hosting ghost tours at the inn recently, so of course Jessie Belle-Blue wanted to do the same. She was all about under-cutting us, but, thankfully, the Gossip Inn had a legacy and over 1,000 positive reviews on TripAdvisor.

Breakfast time arrived, and the guests filled the quaint dining area with its glossy tables, creaking wooden floors, and egg yolk yellow walls. Chatter and laughter leaked through the swinging kitchen doors with their porthole windows.

"That's my cue," I said, dusting off my apron, and heading out into the dining room.

I picked up a pot of coffee from the sideboard where we kept the drinks station and started my rounds.

Most of the guests had gathered around a center table in the dining room, and bursts of laughter came from the group, accompanied by the occasional shout.

I elbowed my way past a couple of guests —nobody could accuse me of having great people skills—apologizing along the way until I reached the table. The last time something like this had happened, a murder had followed shortly afterward.

Not this time. No way.

"—the last thing she'd ever hear!" The

woman seated at the table, drawing the attention, was vaguely familiar. She wore her dark hair in luscious curls, and tossed it as she spoke, looking down her upturned nose at the people around the table.

"What happened then, Mandy?" Another woman asked, her hands clasped together in front of her stomach.

Mandy? Wait a second, isn't this Mandy Gilmore?

Gamma had mentioned her once before—Mandy was a massive gossip in town. Why wasn't she staying at her house?

"What happened? Well, she ran off with her tail between her legs, of course. She'll soon learn not to cross me. Heaven knows, I always repay my debts."

"What, like a Lannister from *Game of Thrones*?" That had come from a taller woman with ginger curls.

"Shut up, Opal," Mandy replied. "You have no idea what we're talking about, and even if you did, you wouldn't have the intelligence to comprehend it."

The crowd let out various 'oofs' in response to that. The woman next to me clapped her hand over her mouth.

"You're all talk, Gilmore." Opal lifted a hand and yammered it at the other woman. "You act like you're a threat, but we know the truth around here."

"The truth?" Mandy leaned in, pressing her hands flat onto the tabletop, the crystal vase in the center rattling. "And what's that, Opal, darling? I'd love to hear it."

"That you're a failure. You sold your house, left Gossip with your head in the clouds, told everyone you were going to become a successful businesswoman, and now you're back. Back to scrape together the pieces of the life you have left."

"Witch!" Mandy scraped her chair back.

"All right, all right," I said, setting down the coffee pot on the table. "That's enough, ladies. Everyone head back to their tables before things get out of hand."

Both Opal and Mandy stared daggers at me.

I flashed them both smiles. "We wouldn't

want to ruin breakfast, would we? Lauren's prepared waffle cupcakes."

That distracted them. "Waffle cupcakes?" Opal's brow wrinkled. "How's that going to work?"

"Let's talk about it at your table." I grabbed my coffee pot and walked her away from Mandy. The crowd slowly dispersed, people muttering regret at having missed out on a show. The Gossip Inn was popular for its constant conflict.

If the rumors didn't start here then they weren't worth repeating. That was the mantra, anyway.

I seated Opal at her table, and she pursed her lips at me. "You shouldn't have interrupted. That woman needs a piece of my mind."

"We prefer peace of mind at the inn." I put up another of my best smiles.

Compared to what I'd been through in the past—hiding out from my rogue spy ex-husband and eventually helping put him behind bars when he found me—dealing with the guests was a cakewalk.

"What brings you to Gossip, Opal?" I asked.

"I live here," she replied, waspishly. "I'm staying here while they're fumigating my house. Roaches."

"Ah." I struggled not to grimace. Thankfully, my cell phone buzzed in the front pocket of my apron and distracted me. "Coffee?"

"I don't take caffeine." And she said it like I'd offered her an illegal substance too.

"Call me if you need anything." I hurried off before she could make good on that promise, bringing my phone out of my pocket.

I left the coffee pot on the sideboard, moving into the Gossip Inn's spacious foyer, the chandelier overhead off, but catching light in glimmers. The tables lining the hall were filled with trinkets from the days when the inn had been a museum—an eclectic collection of bits and bobs.

"This is Charlotte Smith," I answered the call—I would never get to use my true last name, Mission, again, but it was safer this way.

"Hello, Charlotte." A soft, rasping voice.

"I've been trying to get through to you. I'm desperate."

"Who is this?"

"My name is Tina Rogers, and I need your help."

"My help."

"Yes," she said. "I understand that you have a certain set of skills. That you fix people's problems?"

"I do. But it depends on the problem and the price." I didn't have a set fee for helping people, but if it drew me away from the inn for long, I had to charge. I was technically a consultant now. Sort of like a P.I. without the fedora and coffee-stained shirt.

"My mother will handle your fee," Tina said. "I've asked her to text you about it, but I... I don't have long to talk. They're going to pull me off the phone soon."

"Who?"

"The police," she replied. "I'm calling you from the holding cell at the Gossip Police Station. I've been arrested on false charges, and I need you to help me prove my innocence."

"Miss Rogers, it's probably a better idea to

invest in a lawyer." But I was tempted. It had been a long time since I'd felt useful.

"No! I'm not going to a lawyer. I'm going to make these idiots pay for ever having arrested me."

I took a breath. "OK. Before I accept your... case, I'll need to know what happened. You'll need to tell me everything." I glanced through the open doorway that led into the dining room. No one looked unhappy about the lack of service yet.

"I can't tell you everything now. I don't have much time."

"So give me the *CliffsNotes*."

"I was arrested for breaking into and vandalizing Josie Carlson's bakery, The Little Cake Shop. Apparently, they found my glove there—it was specially embroidered, you see —but it's not mine because—" The line went dead.

"Hello? Miss Rogers?" I pulled the cell-phone away from my ear and frowned at the screen. "Darn."

My interest was piqued. A mystery case about a break-in that involved the local bakery? Which just so happened to be run by one of my least favorite people in Gossip?

And when I'd just started getting bored with the push and pull of everyday life at the inn?

Count me in.

🌺   2   🌺

Later that afternoon...

After a successful breakfast service—no one had removed their earrings or choked on a cupcake, proving miracles did happen—I helped Lauren clean up, occasionally checking my phone for texts from Miss Rogers' mother.

They came through thick and fast, along with an offer that dropped my jaw at the sheer number of zeros.

With this kind of money, I could help my grandmother refurbish part of the kitten foster center that was attached to the inn. A necessary requirement now that we'd started converting it into a kitty hotel combo—a place where owners could drop off their cats for care while they went away on vacation or while they stayed at the inn.

Kind of like a kitty daycare.

Business had been good at the inn lately, but not "redo the kitten foster center" good.

"Need anything else from me, Lauren?" I asked, trying not to be too obvious about my excitement over the new "case."

Lauren's sister, Josie, was the owner of The Little Cake Shop which my new client had allegedly broken into. The last thing I wanted was to upset my friend. Even if I despised Josie and all her blustery bossiness.

"Not for now, Charlie," she said. "I'll see you back here in a couple of hours for the service prep."

That was perfect.

It gave me plenty of time to head down to the station and see Tina Rogers before she was transferred to county or saw a judge. Things went slower in Gossip, and that worked out in my favor this time.

"See you later." I stripped off my apron and hung it on a hook next to the kitchen door. I swept out into the hall, my excitement building at the prospect of seeing a new client.

I loved this kind of thing.

The thrill of the chase. The spy-work without the threat of death. And the prospect of wrestling the truth into the light of day.

I couldn't wait to tell my grandmother about it.

"Excuse me! Miss? Excuse me."

Shoot. Freedom was only a few steps away —the sunny exterior of the Gossip Inn, with its fountain, benches, and trees beckoning. My grandmother's Mini-Cooper was parked out front, glinting deep sea-green.

I sighed and turned to the guy who'd called me. "Yes? How may I help you, sir?"

The guy was short and squat, with a pig-gish nose and a set of glasses sliding down it. His name was Brent Grote, and he'd arrived at the inn two days ago. "I have a problem." He lifted a cat and thrust it toward me, scattering fine white powder everywhere.

"Uh?"

"My cat," Mr. Grote said. "I left him in the kitten foster center for care while I went out last night, and this morning, he looks like this."

He waggled the cat. The kitty meowed at me, black face and whiskers speckled white, and his yellow eyes wide.

"Uh... that's odd."

"Odd? Odd? That's my cat you're talking about."

"I know, sir. I meant the dust."

"What is it?" he asked, wrinkling his nose.

"I—can't answer that with confidence," I said. "May I?"

He thrust the cat into my arms. "Somebody's going to pay for this. I need him kept clean for the cat show this week. He's a pedigreed show quality cat."

"I see." I lifted the cat, who meowed again, gormlessly. "Hello there, boy, how are you feeling?"

A blank stare in response.

"Has he been... ill? I'd be happy to take him to the vet if—"

"If he was ill, I wouldn't be having this discussion with you," the man snapped. "He's not ill. He's... ugly."

I barely held back a snort. The irony of that coming from Mr. Grote was, frankly, astounding. Also, I didn't like people who insulted cats.

"Let's see what we've got here." The white powder coated my jeans and t-shirt, but I didn't mind. I pinched some of it off the cat's fur—named Speckles, if his nametag was to be believed—and rubbed it between my fingers.

"What is it? Is it asbestos? I'll sue, I tell you. I'll sue—oh my—what are you doing?"

I had inserted my powder-tipped finger into my mouth. I rolled the flavor around on my tongue, my initial suspicions correct. "It's flour," I said. "He must've gotten into the pantry."

"The pantry! Speckles would never do such a thing, and I resent the insinuation." He took the cat back.

"I wasn't insinuating it so much as saying it

outright," I replied. "I'm sorry about this, Mr. Grote, but there's not much I can do. I suggest you have a chat with Georgina and arrange for a kitty cleaning. She'll be happy to cover the costs. And I'll speak to our chef about pantry security."

Mr. Grote grunted but appeared satisfied by my answer.

Good thing too. I could barely wait to get out of here and speak to Tina Rogers about the bakery break-in, the embroidered glove, and why she didn't want to hire a lawyer to help her with her case.

"You'll need to sign in here, date there, purpose of visit, and all the rest as indicated there," the police officer, Miller, said, lazily. He fingered a line on a fresh page. "And then I'm going to have to conduct a search. For contraband."

"Fine," I said, hurriedly scratching a pen over the page. The Gossip Police Station was a dreary place, with white tiles, old wooden counters, and gray walls, but it was neatly kept. Often, smaller towns had better budgets for policing compared to their city counterparts.

"If you'll step this way, ma'am," Officer Miller said, gesturing off to the side of the desk. "I'm going to search you now, and then I'll let Miss Rogers know that she has a visitor and take her to the visitation area."

I did as he'd asked, allowing him to check that I had nothing that could be passed through to Tina, my patience waning by the second. Officer Miller grunted his satisfaction, then exited the room through an open archway. His footsteps squeaked on the tiles, and I checked my watch.

I'd have to be back at the inn soon, especially if I wanted to ask Lauren about the pantry and how a cat had gotten in there, before we started preparing for the dinner service. I hadn't even gotten around to my dusting for the day.

A shout rang from the holding cell area.

"Officer Miller?" I frowned and peeked through the doorway.

The room beyond it was large and open, with brown counters lining the walls, blue plastic bins beneath them. Off to one side was an area with red lines demarcated on the tiles —where mugshots were taken—and in the corner was what I could only describe as a cage.

Officer Miller was in the process of unlocking the cage's door, fumbling around with his keys, one hand on his radio as he called for help.

Tina Rogers lay supine, staring sightlessly at the ceiling, her hand open, the scattered crumbs of a chocolate brownie on the floor next to her.

3

The interrogation room's door slammed shut behind the detective. He walked over to the table that had been shoved into the corner, and sat down, producing two bottles of water.

New guy. I'd been so involved in life at the inn the past few months, I hadn't even registered that the detective who'd investigated the previous murder cases was gone. Detective Crowley had retired, and this young man, I said young, but he was probably around the same age as me—mid-thirties—had to be his replacement.

Neatly trimmed black hair and sharp, green eyes set in a masculine face. Strong jawline. Handsome, even though it didn't matter to me. I'd been through too much with men, already. No more dating. And no more ex-husbands, thank you very much.

"Miss Smith," he said, offering me a white-toothed smile. His teeth weren't perfectly straight, but that added to his charm. "My name is Detective Aaron Goode. Are you comfortable? Happy?"

"I wouldn't say happy, but sure. I'm comfortable. I did just see a dead body."

Detective Goode flipped open the brown paper file he'd brought in. "It seems you've got some experience with dead bodies."

"Uh... should I be complimented by that?" *Remember, Charlie, you're a maid. You're not meant to know anything about anything.*

Goode's lips twitched upward at the corners. "I've got a record here from my predecessor, Detective Crowley, that mentions your involvement in several cases. It's interesting. Seems like you've been everywhere and nowhere all at once." He shut the folder. "Why is that?"

"No reason is particular," I replied. " I'm a maid at the Gossip Inn. But, I'm curious, Detective Goode, why are *you* here?"

"Meaning?"

"It's a small town," I said. "Even when Detective Crowley was here, I wondered why Gossip saw fit to have a detective around."

"It's with the town's best interests at heart given the uptick in murders around here lately."

"There hasn't been an incident in nine months," I said, coolly.

I wasn't usually like this. I tried to maintain my friendly, wilting maid cover, but there was something about Detective Goode muscling in on my territory that got under my skin. And his line of questioning wasn't setting me at ease either.

"Exactly nine months," Goode said, examining me with a tilted head. "You've been keeping track of the time?"

"Look, I'm sure you're just doing your job, but you can't seriously think that I had anything to do with Tina Rogers' death. Ask Officer Miller where I was when he found her, if you'd like."

"Don't worry what I think, Miss Smith," Goode said. "I'd like to ask you a few questions about what you saw today."

"Sure. Go ahead." *Calm down, for heaven's sake. He's doing his job. And you have an alibi.*

"Let's start from the beginning. Why did you come to see Miss Rogers today?"

"She asked to see me."

"Why?"

"Because she needed my help with her arrest."

"Her arrest?"

Oh boy, this was going to go down a treat. "Yes," I replied. "She wanted my help proving that she had been wrongfully arrested. She claimed that she hadn't broken into The Little Cake Shop and that the embroidered glove found on the scene wasn't hers."

"And why would she ask for your help?" Detective Goode asked.

"Because I like helping people."

He waited for more, but I didn't offer it.

The cream colored walls and the stark floors should've made me uneasy, but I'd been in worse situations than this. Worse interrogations.

"So, you came down here to talk to her about her case."

"Yeah."

"And then what happened?"

"I didn't get to talk to her." I told him everything, from my arrival and signing in, to when the body had been discovered. "And that's it, I have no idea what happened." *Probably poisoning, what with the brownie on the floor and all.*

Detective Goode stared at me in silence.

"Do you know who else was visiting her this morning?" I asked. "Because that's where I'd start my list of suspects if I were you." If only I'd caught a glimpse of the sign in sheet. I'd written my details on a fresh page.

"Thanks for the advice, Miss Smith," Goode said. "But I can take it from here."

"Ah. Right. Sure." I hoped he was right because the last detective who'd worked cases in this town sure hadn't been able to handle it.

Not that it mattered. I had no choice but to get involved this time around.

Tina's mother had already transferred half the cash to clear her daughter's name into my account, and I had a feeling that she would want me to figure out what had happened in the holding cell. Of course, I'd have to get hold of her first, after she'd been informed of her daughter's passing, but regardless...

"Is that all you need from me, Detective?"

Goode scanned his notepad, his handwriting neat and blocky in blue ink. "Do you know of anyone who might've wanted to harm Miss Rogers?"

"Say, I was wondering that myself," I replied. "But no. I don't." I intended to find out. I'd been given the gift of purpose, and I wasn't about to let go of the opportunity. "She mentioned Josie Carlson from The Little Cake Shop on the phone." What would the motive be, though? Josie wouldn't have a clear-cut reason to harm Tina.

You don't know that yet. Find out more about what happened first.

"Detective, why was Tina arrested? Was it

just the glove that suggested she was the one who had robbed the bakery?"

"That's part of an open investigation, Miss Smith. I can't share that information with you."

"Oh." I acted shocked. "Then what can you share with me?"

"I can share with you the time of day," he replied, as cool as I'd been earlier. Cool as a slice of no-bake cheesecake. "And that you don't need to worry about helping Miss Rogers anymore. That's in the hands of the Gossip Police now."

"I'm sure she would've appreciated that," I replied, sweetly.

Goode raised an eyebrow at me before scanning his page of notes again. He pushed me a few more times, making me walk through exactly what had happened, but treating me as a witness. He hadn't read me my rights, so I was free to go after another twenty minutes of prodding and cajoling.

I exited the Gossip Police Station, cell phone in hand, my gaze on the screen. Poor Mrs. Rogers would find out soon enough what had happened, if she hadn't already. Regardless of whether she wanted me to investigate or not, I needed to find out what had happened.

I couldn't let this lie. Nothing would stop me from ensuring no ill befell this town.

4

My grandmother and I met at our rendezvous point in the front yard, both for an update on what she'd discovered at Jessie Belle-Blue's new guesthouse, and to discuss what had happened with Tina. It was a lovely sunny afternoon, birds chirping in the trees, and the day warm but not too hot. Not that I could appreciate it on a day like this.

"Fascinating," Gamma said, seated on a bench under one of the many trees in the Gossip Inn's grounds. "A brownie?"

"Yeah. Brownie. I'm sure of it."

"A baked good kills a woman who broke into a bakery." Gamma paused. "And that woman also owned a bakery herself."

"Wait, back up a second. Tina Rogers owned a bakery too?" I asked.

"Correct. Specializing in breads of every kind. People like their baked goods in this town. Comforting food is a winner when there's not much to do except sweat and gossip."

Truer words had never been spoken. "I wonder why she didn't tell me that," I said. "Then again, she didn't have time. She got cut off."

"Did her mother mention it?"

"I haven't heard from her yet. I assume she's been busy with the police."

Gamma fell silent, her hawkish blue eyes focused on a point in the distance. "But you're curious, aren't you? About who did this?"

"Georgina," I replied, "do you even need to ask?" I had to call my grandmother Georgina in front of other people, and I'd gotten into the habit. We couldn't risk exposing our true identities. Gamma had a lot of enemies from her past.

"Then what are you going to do, Charlotte?" Gamma asked. "What avenues will you investigate?"

My grandmother would be with me every step of the way. While she coped with the molasses trickle of life in Gossip by investing in side projects—the inn, the kitten foster center —she still enjoyed dabbling in mysteries with me.

"This bakery thing interests me. So Tina owned a bakery, yes?"

"Correct."

"And so did Josie." I grimaced. I wasn't a fan of Josie Carlson, though I kept our relationship civil for Lauren, the inn's chef's sake. "And Tina was accused of breaking into said bakery and... what? Why? Did she steal something?"

"According to my grapevine," Gamma said, referring to her many friends and gossip buddies in town, "Josie's bakery was vandalized."

"Who told you that?" I asked.

"A lady never rats out her informants, Charlotte." Gamma fluttered long eyelashes at me. "But it was Lauren. Obviously."

"Right, OK. Vandalism. Locked up for vandalism? There's got to be more to it than that."

"Things went missing too," Gamma said. "Theft and vandalism. I don't have all the details."

"I'll have to get them from Josie." *Perish the thought.* "She'll know what's going on, and, as of now, she's my prime suspect." I ticked off points on my fingers. "Her bakery was allegedly vandalized by Tina, who claimed that she wasn't the one whodunit, and Tina was murdered by a poisoned brownie."

"You're assuming that," Gamma replied. "It's not as if you've received a toxicology report. How much of the body did you see?"

"I got a brief glimpse of the brownie, her hand, and her face. Officer Miller was blocking everything else from view."

"Then you don't know for certain that it was poisoning, do you?"

"You're right," I said.

That complicated things. If Tina hadn't been poisoned, my suspect pool opened up, but I was curious about who had visited her. And how she had died.

"But who could've done this without Officer Miller overhearing?" I asked. "If it wasn't poisoning by crumbly brownie then it had to have been a violent death. And violence begets noise. Wouldn't Miller have heard or checked on Tina after the last visitor?"

"That I can't say," Gamma replied. "He'll have the answer to that."

"Right," I said, and fished my cell phone out of the pocket of my jeans. I opened a fresh note.

Victim Name: *Tina Rogers.*

Victim Detail: *Baker. In legal trouble. Hired me to prove her innocence—accused of breaking into The Little Cake Shop owned by Josie Carlson.*

Cause of Death: *Murder. Weapon unknown. Potentially poisoning. Confirmation required.*

Suspects

Josie Carlson

???

Evidence

Glove embroidered specially for Tina found in Josie's bakery.

Brownie at crime scene.

Links

Josie owned a bakery. Brownie was found next to the victim's hand.

Tina's glove was found in Josie's bakery. Tina claimed the glove wasn't hers.

Someone who visited Tina must've killed her.

Connection of Tina's "crime" to the murder?

Questions

Who visited Tina at the holding cells before me?

Who baked the brownies?

Did the brownies contain poison?

What was the cause of death?

What did Officer Miller hear?

Who was the owner of the glove found in Josie's bakery?

"I can handle that one for you." Gamma pointed at the first question listed. "I'll find out who visited Tina in the holding cells."

"Great. Thanks, Georgina."

"But of course."

I closed my app and rose from the bench, mentally prepping for what I had to do next. Talk to Josie about the glove, the break-in, and whether she saw Tina this morning.

Have mercy.

5

The Little Cake Shop was tucked off Gossip's Main Street in Baker Avenue, a name that was steeped in history. It seemed that all the coffee shops and bakeries—of which there were many—were tucked into this street and had been for years.

Delicious smells of bread and confectionery drifted on the air. It was like I'd stepped into "Diagon Alley" for bakers.

My stomach grumbled, but I ignored it and scanned the outside of The Little Cake Shop.

A brick building, with plenty of windows

letting in natural light, a glass front door with a cartoon cake logo on the front, the look completed by the cream and baby blue striped awning, bearing the bakery's name in golden print.

Inviting. But the sign in the front door read CLOSED in big bold letters.

I walked up to it, cupping my hands either side of my face, and peered inside.

A woman stared back at me from within. Short, brunette, plump and unfriendly, Josie raised an eyebrow.

I jerked back, sucking in a breath. *There's a sight you don't see every day. And don't want to.* "Josie," I called, and rapped my knuckles on the glass. "Mind if I talk to you for a second?"

The door opened, bell tinkling above it. Josie blocked my entry, her eyebrow stuck in an annoyed arch. "I know you," she said, sniffing. "You're Lauren's friend, right? The maid at the inn."

"That's right. Charlotte. Or Charlie. Whichever you prefer." She had to remember me. We'd spent a day in the kitchen together while she looked after Lauren's firstborn not too long ago. But she was one of those types of people. The kind who pretended they didn't remember you because it made them feel special.

"What do you want?" she asked. "I'm in the middle of cleaning up."

"I had a couple of questions for you," I said. "On behalf of Tina Rogers."

That took the wind right out of her snobby sails. The eyebrow sank back into a natural position. "T-Tina?"

"That's right," I said, offering her a bright smile. "I assume you heard about what happened in the holding cells?"

Josie swallowed audibly. "Yeah. I heard. So what?"

"So, Tina's dead, but before she passed, she asked me to help her clear her name. You accused her of breaking into your store."

"It was pretty obvious it was her. She left her glove behind. She never takes those gloves off. She even carries them with her in summer. I bet she thought she'd leave fingerprints behind or... I don't know, something, and she wore the gloves to hide her identity while she was ruining my shop."

"So, you're suggesting she dropped a glove even though she was using them to hide her identity, and thus was identified by it?"

"Why did she ask *you* for help?"

"I think you know why." It was common knowledge that I'd been involved in solving a few mysteries.

"Whatever. What do you want to know?"

"First, what happened here?" I asked. "What did Tina take from your store?"

Josie didn't invite me in, and I didn't expect her to. A couple of people passed by on the sidewalk, and Josie waited before answering. "There was some money missing from the register, not that much, and she trashed the place."

"Trashed it how?"

"Spray paint, broken chairs, glass, that kind of thing. I got the paint off, but this is costing me a fortune to repair. And being closed doesn't help either. My customers love my offerings, and they're upset about this too."

Yeah, definitely an arrestable offense. "Why did you think it was Tina?"

"I told you. The glove. The stupid, pink glove with the daisy embroidered on the front. It was made specially for her."

"OK," I said.

Interesting that Josie was willing to answer my questions. Was she trying to appear innocent?

"And where did she get this glove?" I asked.

"No idea," Josie replied. "Why would I know that? We weren't exactly the best of friends. She was annoying, always talking about bread. Who cares about bread? Not me. And, uh, yeah, all I know is that she kept bragging that her gloves were specially made. She never told me who had made them though."

I nodded. "Uh-huh. OK. And when did you last see Tina?" I asked.

Josie checked her watch. "How much longer do you want to talk for? I'm busy."

"The more information you give me the

better," I said. "It's all in aid of finding out who broke into your store."

Josie let out a breath, like she'd rather be doing anything other than talking to me. "A couple of days ago."

"A couple of days ago," I repeated, searching her face. "You're sure about that."

"Yeah." She glanced off to the right. "Yeah. Why?"

"Just curious."

"I have to go. I have things to do, and this is a fantastic waste of my time." Josie shut the door in my face and turned the lock with a resounding *click*.

I backed up a few steps on the sidewalk, folding my arms over my cotton, sleeveless blouse, and peering up at the sign overhead.

I don't buy it. There's something fishy going on here.

🎇 6 🎇

That evening...

Lauren finished loading the last of the dishes into the dishwasher, humming under her breath. I sat at the rough wooden table in the Gossip Inn's kitchen, my case notes open on my phone, and my brow furrowed. I kept a hand on Tyson's stroller, where he dozed—the little tyke had turned one not long ago, and had a bubbly attitude to match his mother's.

Thank goodness he didn't inherit any personality traits from his aunt, Josie.

"Figured anything out yet?" Lauren asked.

"Nothing yet. I've got clues but no answers. Of course, I've just started looking into it so... It will be a while before I have anything concrete."

"Have you heard from Tina's mother?"

"Yeah, actually. She asked me to meet her tomorrow morning to talk about everything. She wants me to clear Tina's name, and, I'm guessing, figure out who did this. But we'll see what happens. Either way, I'm checking it out."

"We can always count on you, Charlie." Lauren wiped her hands off on her apron. "Look at him, sleeping like an angel." She sighed. "I hope it stays that way. He's been fussy lately. I think it's got to do with the ghost."

I blinked, shifting my gaze from the phone to my friend. "The what?"

"The ghost. In my basement."

Lauren was a big believer in the supernatural. I was a believer in facts. And that there was usually a rational, sometimes nefarious, reason for supposedly paranormal events. I wasn't about to judge Lauren for her beliefs.

"Why do you think there's a ghost in your basement?" I asked.

"Noises at night. And it's not animals or rats or whatever. Oh, Charlie, don't look at me like that, I'm serious. There's a ghost in the basement. I hear it howling at night, and I'm pretty sure that's what's keeping Tyke awake."

"You know," I said, returning to my case notes. "Pregnancy hormones give you vivid dreams. It's a scientific fact."

"They also give me mood swings," Lauren said. "Do you really want to get on the wrong side of a hormonal woman with easy access to knives and a rolling pin?"

"Merely making an observation." I grinned at her.

A meow sounded from the kitchen doorway.

Cocoa Puff, the inn's resident cat, chocolate fur and a sweet disposition, sat in the hallway, looking in. All cats were forbidden from entering the kitchen, and they stuck to the rules for fear of the chef's wrath—a spritz from a spray bottle full of water.

"Hey, boy," I cooed, and got up from the chair. I walked out into the hall and stroked Cocoa Puff. "I missed you today." Usually I was in the inn, cleaning or serving guests, with Cocoa Puff tailing close behind. He was a great companion and alternated between sleeping at the base of my bed or my grandmother's.

Ever since I'd adopted a new cat, Sunlight, a boisterous ginger boy who liked getting up to mischief, Cocoa Puff had taken to switching up his attention between me, Gamma, and the guests.

A *prrrt* was followed by the appearance of Sunlight, himself. He ran up the hall and bumped into my leg, purring like mad.

"Hey, and there you—oh!" Sunlight's fur was covered in a fine coating of white dust.

Shoot! I forgot about the flour from this morning.

"Hey, Laur, come look at this for a second, will you?"

Lauren turned the stroller around,

checking Tyson was still asleep, then came over to us. "What is it?"

"Flour on Sunlight's fur." I drew my fingers through his ginger fur and held them aloft. "See? Mr. Grote came to me this morning with his cat covered in flour too. I told him we'd check on pantry security. Is the pantry door locked?"

"Of course," Lauren said. "Always. And there's no window in there. No way one of the cats could've gotten in. Gosh, there's hardly enough flour to go around to get them messy in the first place."

"Weird."

"Besides, wasn't Mr. Grote's cat in the kitten foster center?" Lauren nodded toward the door that separated the main portion of the inn from the kitten foster center. It was an engraved, thick wooden door, kept locked at all times. Only Gamma, Lauren, and I had keys for it.

"You're right. This is super strange." I dusted off Sunlight's fur, carefully. He purred, appreciating the extra grooming help. "I wonder how it happened."

"I don't know, but it didn't come from my pantry. You know I run a tight ship, Charlie," Lauren said, in her Texas twang.

"I know."

Lauren returned to the kitchen to clean the last of the counters—her favorite thing to do before she left for the evening—and I got to thinking. Not so much about the floury fur, that was a mystery that could wait, but about Tina and, especially, Josie.

I gave Sunlight and Cocoa Puff a kiss apiece on their heads, then entered the kitchen. "I spoke to your sister today."

"Oh! About the break-in at the bakery?"

"Yeah," I replied. "And about Tina. I had a question—how well did Josie and Tina know each other?"

Lauren stopped wiping down the counters and fisted her hips. "Well, now, Charlie, why are you asking? Surely, you don't think my sister had anything to do with what happened to Tina."

"I'm not saying that," I replied, trying for diplomacy. "I'm collecting as much information as possible about the victim and her relationships with others. If Josie knew a lot about Tina's life, she might tell me who didn't like her."

"Oh. Yeah, sure. I get that." Lauren returned to her scrubbing. "Tina and Jo go *way* back. They were in the same year at high school together, you know? Kind of like... frenemies, but more friends than enemies. Josie always wanted the best for her. She was real excited when Tina opened up The Bread Factory. They talked a lot about doing a joint venture together."

"That's cool. So they were friends. On good terms?"

"Yeah, definitely."

Then why did Josie tell me they weren't? And why did I get the feeling that Josie had something to hide?

"That's good news. I'll talk to her again sometime. I think she was flustered today."

"Oh, yeah," Lauren said. "She's been dealing with a lot lately. The break-in, boyfriend stuff, and now Tina dying."

"Poor Josie." Through divine intervention, it seemed, I managed to keep the sarcasm from my voice. "How are she and your husband getting on?" Jason was another person I didn't like much. I considered him a deadbeat dad. When Lauren had first had Tyke, Jason had lied to her and hidden out for weeks at a time because he needed "space" while she dealt with her newborn. They were still together. Another case of divine intervention. Or, rather, marriage counseling.

"Oh, as usual. Josie and Jason can't stand each other." Lauren rolled her eyes. "But it doesn't matter to me. I've got my boy and a baby on the way. I don't have time for family drama."

"Good to hear." I helped Lauren with the last of the cleaning, waved goodbye to a groggy Tyson in his stroller, then exited into the hall, the cats on my heels.

Tomorrow can't come soon enough.

There was murder and mystery afoot.

7

The following morning...

Tina's mother, Mrs. Ursula Rogers, met me outside the Hungry Steer— the most popular restaurant in Gossip. The Steer was housed in a big red barn, with all the trappings expected of a place with its appearance, including hay bales, rough hewn tables, barrel stands, and lanterns for lighting.

Mrs. Rogers was the older version of her

daughter. Blonde, tall, and willowy, with a pretty face, and an unfortunately large nose to add character to it.

"Thank you for meeting with me this morning, Mrs. Rogers," I said, emerging from my Gamma's sea-green Mini-Cooper.

We shook hands. Mrs. Rogers' shake was firm, but her eyes were puffy.

"I'm sorry it's under these circumstances," I said.

"Please. Don't thank me. I'm the one who needs your help. I should be thanking you," she said, her voice catching in her throat.

"There's nothing to thank me for yet." I gestured to the Hungry Steer. "Shall we?"

We entered the homey interior and were seated at one of the booths near the back of the restaurant. Mrs. Rogers wore black and toyed with the menu, looking around the place.

"It's busy," she said. "This early in the morning?"

"Oh sure," I replied. "Grayson Tombs, the owner, likes to keep his employees working around the clock." Needless to say, Grayson was another person I didn't like. He flirted inappropriately with Lauren and had insulted my grandmother to boot.

Hmm. There are a lot of people I don't like, apparently.

We ordered our drinks—a coffee for Mrs. Rogers and a strawberry milkshake for me—then settled into the booth.

"I'm sorry for your loss, Mrs. Rogers," I said. "I didn't know Tina well, but she seemed like a nice person from the short call we had. I'll understand if you'd like me to give up the investigation and return your funds."

"No! No, please. I don't want that. I need you to figure out what's going on here." Mrs. Rogers welled up. "My daughter was murdered in a holding cell. You can't tell me that it's a coincidence. I mean, first she's arrested on trumped up charges that make no sense, and then this happens? The police have to be involved. Or... someone is. I don't know. I'm confused."

"Have you spoken to Detective Goode?"

"Yes. And he wasn't exactly forthcoming about his investigation. He asked me questions about Tina's friends and enemies and that was it. He didn't offer me any information. It's so annoying."

"My experience was similar." Detective Goode was just doing his job. Still, it was kind of annoying not being able to twist his arm like I had with the previous detective.

Mrs. Rogers drank her coffee in silence.

"Mrs. Rogers, if you want me to help you, I'm going to need to ask you a couple of questions. I know this isn't the best time but—"

She waved a hand. "I'll answer any questions you have. Whatever helps you find who did this to my daughter."

"All right." I removed my phone from my purse. I placed it on the table and unlocked it, opening it to my case notes. "I'll be taking some notes while we talk. Is that OK with you?"

"Yes, of course."

"Mrs. Rogers, Tina mentioned an embroidered glove that was found in Josie's bakery. Can you tell me about that? Do you know where she got the gloves? And whether it was the only pair of its kind?"

"Yes, they were definitely special. Mary Moosmin from the Gossip Sewing Club made the pair of gloves for her years ago. They were light, since most of our winters have been light, but they were beautiful and comfortable. Tina loved them. She didn't go anywhere without them, which was why it was such a shock to her when one of her gloves was found in Josie's bakery."

"Tina mentioned that the glove wasn't hers on the phone. Did she say anything like that to you?"

Mrs. Rogers shook her head. "No. That was Tina's glove. I've brought the other one along for you for evidence purposes." She removed it from her handbag and placed it on the table.

I took it, carefully, and turned it over. *Yep. It's a pink glove, with a daisy embroidered on the front. Orange floral disc.*

"Thank you," I said. "This is helpful. I wonder why Tina said it wasn't her glove if these were made specially for her."

"I don't know, but I can't find the other one, so it must be her glove. Right? That's why we were so shocked when she was arrested. Tina's never let her gloves out of her sight. She takes them with her everywhere, even during the summer."

"Why?"

"She has a special connection with them." Mrs. Rogers' smile was soft. "She *had* a special connection with them. Every time I asked why, she would dodge the question. She was... my eccentric little girl. Young woman." She pinched her eyes closed and took a breath. "Sorry. I need a minute."

I examined the inside of the glove and the fabric, but it was like asking a brick wall for an omen. I tucked it into my purse for safe keeping.

"Can you tell me anything about Tina's friendships? Relationships, maybe? A boyfriend?"

"Oh no. No. Tina was very business-focused. She didn't have a boyfriend. And friends? She had a lot of them. She was sort of friends with Josie, but that's kind of on and off. I don't know, you know how women can be. Changeable. Especially Josie. I can't believe she had my Tina arrested. That she'd even think Tina would try to vandalize her bakery... Tina was the one who suggested a joint venture with Josie. Why would she jeopardize that?"

So, that's two people who have disputed Josie's account of their friendship. Interesting.

I made a note of it. "This is an awkward question, but can you think of anyone who might've wanted to harm Tina? Is there anything or anyone that springs to mind as suspicious?"

Mrs. Rogers turned her cup in a circle between her palms. "No," she said. "Apart from the police arresting her and Josie's change of heart, no. I can't think of anything or anyone that was different this past week."

Not exactly the lead I had hoped for.

So far, all the evidence pointed squarely at Josie. *Lauren's not going to be happy about this.*

8

"That horrible creature at *The Gossip Rag* has been spreading rumors about you, Charlotte." Gamma sat at the kitchen table, wearing a Gossip Inn apron, shelling peas into a silver bowl. Lauren was behind the stove, cooking up a storm.

I had just gotten back from my meeting with Mrs. Rogers, a whirl of questions sweeping through my mind. "What do you mean?" I removed my apron from the hook next to the kitchen door and slipped it on. "What's Jacinta saying now?"

Jacinta Redgrave had the scruples of a

starving carrion bird when it came to gossip and news. I didn't blame her, what with printed news being a dying industry and all, but it was annoying that Gamma and I always got the short end of the stick.

"You're a suspect," Gamma said. "According to public opinion, at least. I'm unsure of Detective Goode's areas of investigation currently." She *pinged* another pea from the pod into the bowl. "But I'll find out. My grapes are listening."

I wasn't about to stress out over Detective Goode's investigation yet. If he came knocking, well, then I'd worry, but for now, I had bigger problems to fix.

Lauren hummed a country song under her breath.

"Where do you need me?" I asked her.

"Finely chopped onions, please." She gestured with her spoon.

"Oh, joy." I grabbed my onion goggles—a pair of repurposed ski goggles—from their drawer and put them on. The world got a little hazier. These things were old.

Once I'd gotten the onions, chopping

board, and knife onto the table and taken my seat, Gamma cleared her throat.

"I found some information you might deem interesting," she said, with another choice ping of a pea.

"Lay it on me." I brandished my knife, dreading the first cut into the onion. The goggles usually worked, but they had their limits, and Lauren had set out six onions for dicing.

"I spoke to Mary-Ellen at the police station," Gamma said. "She managed to, uh, procure that list you were looking for."

"Are you serious?" I asked. "How did you convince her to give you that information?"

The list of people who had visited Tina Rogers. This would be helpful. I could fully furnish my suspect list at last! Investigations weren't easy—I'd been a spy in my past life, not a detective, so I was following the path of least resistance here.

"Oh, a cake or two. And I gave her a coupon for a free ghost tour next month," Gamma said. "We need to start testing the tours out properly. Come up with new information to lure in more takers."

"What did Mary-Ellen tell you?"

"Tina Rogers had three visitors, excluding you, on the morning of her murder."

"So many. And Officer Miller let them all see her?"

"Apparently," Gamma replied. "It's Gossip, Charlotte. Miller likely let a lot of things slip beneath the radar. Or under the table."

"Meaning we could pay him off with ghost tour tickets?"

Gamma shot me a secretive smile.

"So, who were the three visitors?"

"This is where it gets interesting," she said. "They were, in chronological order, Josie Carlson, Mandy Gilmore, and Bridget Willows."

"Mandy Gilmore. She's staying at the inn."

"Indeed," Gamma said, in her prim British accent. "Only recently returned after leaving for greener pastures."

I set down my knife and brought out my phone, blinking behind the ski goggles. I tapped through to my case notes and added the three names to the suspects list.

"What do we know about Bridget Willows?" I asked.

"She's the head of the Gossip Sewing Club," Lauren said, instantly. "She's a lovely woman. When Josie and I were girls, she'd babysit for our momma when she needed to get out of the house to run errands. She was so patient with us too, even though Josie had the tendency to raise heck."

I had kept my opinions about Josie under wraps, but the fact that she'd visited Tina on the morning of the murder, after telling me that she hadn't seen her for days, was beyond suspicious.

But I wasn't about to bring that up in front of Lauren.

"OK, interesting. That's the second time the Gossip Sewing Club has been mentioned to me today," I replied, and briefly told my grandmother about what Mrs. Rogers had said. "I think I'll have to talk to this Bridget Willows lady soon."

"You'll love her," Lauren said, brightly. "She's an angel. Charlie, would you watch my sauce for a second? I've got to run to the ladies room."

"Sure. No problem." I set my phone aside,

pulled up my ski goggles, and walked over to the stovetop.

Lauren rushed out, breezing past Cocoa Puff who lay across the doorway, drifting in and out of dreams.

"Now that she's gone," Gamma said, immediately. "What about Josie?"

"She's a liar," I replied. "She told me two lies. First, that she and Tina weren't friends, and, second, that she hadn't seen her for days before the murder."

"Perhaps, only one of those is a lie."

Given that we *knew* Josie had dropped by the station to see Tina, it was clear what my grandmother meant. Josie might not have been friends with Tina. Not anymore.

I watched the sauce like a hawk. It simmered peacefully, no smoke in sight—but I didn't trust it. Food tended to burn the minute I looked away, and I didn't need a hormonal Lauren breathing down my neck because of it.

"She's my target," I said. "Though, I might talk to Mandy Gilmore first because she's, you know, right here in the inn."

Lauren re-entered the kitchen and bustled over. She stirred the sauce, tasted it, and eyed me. "Good," she said. "You didn't burn it this time."

"Not through my own doing," I replied. "It was sheer luck."

I put my goggles on then dropped into my chair and grabbed my knife. I had onions to chop and a killer to find. Especially, if Detective Goode had decided I was to blame for Tina's death. Even if he didn't, I wasn't about to subject the people of Gossip to a murderer on the loose.

"Careful, Charlotte, you'll slice a finger off chopping like this."

"Excuse me," I replied. "This is Gordon Ramsey's technique. I watched a video and everything."

"He must look fetching in ski goggles."

I rolled my eyes at my grandmother and nearly sliced off my finger. "You're distracting me, see?"

Gamma returned to shelling her peas, a sneaky smile parting her lips. And me? Well, I returned to my rumination.

Why had Josie lied to me? What had Mandy Gilmore, the infamous returning gossip, been doing at the station on the morning of the murder? And why on earth was the Gossip Sewing Club involved in this?

Inquiring spies deserved to know.

❧ 9 ❧

After lunch, I abandoned Lauren to her cleaning of the kitchen and exited into the hallway, heading for the closet that kept my favorite cleaning supply. The feather duster. Not only was the feather duster a fun way to keep Sunlight and Cocoa Puff entertained, but it was a low stress cleaning activity.

Dusting trinkets and tables in the inn's many nooks and crannies was a lot more fun than cleaning windows or vacuuming or polishing the floors. It was the perfect way to look busy without actually being busy.

Gamma saw right through the ruse. But, eh, she let me get away with it. And I needed the time to think today.

I dusted the crystal ball on the trinket table under my grandmother's antique mirror, considering the evidence so far.

Mandy Gilmore, newly returned, had visited Tina. Were they old friends, maybe? Or was there another, more wicked reason for the visit?

And what about Josie and her lies? I didn't want to put my friend, Lauren in a precarious and uncomfortable position, but I wouldn't put murder past Josie. She had it in the eyes. Kind of. OK, not really, but she was bossy, mean, and wasn't it true that just about everybody had the potential to be a killer?

What about the Gossip Sewing Club and—?

"Knock, knock." The deep voice rumbled from the inn's doors.

I jolted then reprimanded myself. I'd quit being a spy about nine months ago. The time it took to gestate a human being had seen the loss of my usual sense of perpetual awareness. Disappointing.

I turned to the door. "Oh. Hello."

Detective Goode, wearing a neat buttoned shirt and a pair of plain blue slacks, stood on the threshold. He straightened the lanyard that bore his badge. "How are you today, Miss Smith?" he asked, stiffly.

Man, he's cute.

"I'm fine, thank you," I replied. "How are you?" Internally, I measured that my tone was calm but not devoid of emotion, all the while trying to track his movements.

Was he here to talk to me?

"Good. Hot and busy, you could say."

"May I help you with something, Detective?" I twirled the feather duster then tucked it under my arm. "Do you not have a place to stay in town?"

"I do, thank you, Miss Smith. I'm here to see one of your guests. I've been told that Miss Mandy Gilmore is staying here. That correct?"

"Yeah, that's right," I replied. "I can get her for you, if you'd like."

"That would be peachy."

Peachy? Who even says peachy?

"Please, take a seat in the dining room. I'll go up and fetch her." I gestured toward the dining area.

"Sure, will do. Thank you." He strolled past me, wafting cologne that was lemony and light, then took a seat at a center most table, his back to the door.

Interrogation technique. He's putting himself between the door and his target, once she sits down. But why wouldn't he ask her to come down to the station then? Maybe, he was following up on a loose end that needed tying.

I proceeded up to the second floor, where Mandy Gilmore was staying in the Rose Room, and knocked.

A burst of complaints sounded, followed by footsteps and the creak of the door. "I don't need my room cleaned, thank you," Mandy said. "It was cleaned yesterday." She gestured to the "Do Not Disturb" sign hanging off the doorknob. "Can't you read? I'm trying to take a nap here."

Don't punch a guest. Never punch a guest, Charlie. "I'm so sorry to interrupt, Miss Gilmore," I said, trying the obsequious approach. "But

Detective Goode is downstairs, and he's asked to talk to you."

Mandy frowned. "Oh. Oh, OK. Well, why didn't you say so?"

I ignored the jibe and stepped back, allowing her to exit her room. I followed close on her heels, feather duster and all.

Mandy tossed her dark curls, giving me the side-eye as we entered the dining room. "Hello, Detective. You wanted to see me?"

"Please, take a seat."

"Can I get you guys anything to drink?" I asked. "Lemonade?"

"I'm fine, thank you," Mandy said.

"Nothing for me, thanks."

"Holler if you need anything." And with that, I left them to it.

Or so they thought.

Really, I dipped around the corner and continued my dusting—faking my cleaning duties now more than ever. My ears would've been pricked up if I were a cat.

"—follow up—a few things." Detective Goode's voice.

Darn it, I needed to get closer. I shifted

up, my breathing calm and practiced. The awareness I'd lacked earlier had resurged in force.

"—what more there is to say. I wanted to come here and be with the family—"

"—understand. Did Tina know him?"

"Quite well."

"—and she was going to attend the funeral as well?" Detective Goode asked, lightly.

"—chance to talk to her about that, specifically."

"Then what did you get the chance to—"

"Mainly the past. Friend stuff."

A short silence from Detective Goode followed. "I think that's all for now. But I'll be in touch if anything comes up." He talked louder, as if the tension between them had broken and he could talk more freely.

"Thanks, Detective Goode. I appreciate you're in a difficult position. I know you're doing everything you can to find out the truth." Mandy's voice was louder too, and she simpered at the detective, as if that would help her.

Maybe it would. I hadn't sussed out what type of man Goode was yet.

I retreated, stealthily, and dipped into the kitchen with my feather duster.

Lauren sipped from a cup at the kitchen table. "I've been craving this stuff every day since the second trimester of my pregnancy started," she said.

"What is it?" I asked because talking to her and being heard would allay suspicions. Mandy and Detective Goode would hardly think I'd listened in if they knew I was in here with Lauren.

"Boiling water with slices of cucumber and lemon, a sprinkle of cinnamon on top."

"Gross!"

"I know," Lauren said, and took another sip. "But the baby wants it. And what the baby wants, the baby gets."

"Excuse me." Detective Goode spoke from the hall outside the kitchen.

"Oh, hello, Detective," Lauren said, happily. "Would you like a cup of tea? Coffee?"

"Boiled water with cucumber slices, lemon, and cinnamon?" I added in.

Detective Goode pulled a face. "Hard pass. Thanks. Can I talk to you for a moment, Miss Smith?" He crooked a finger at me, and I was tempted to grab it and twist it around. Crooking a finger? Rude.

"Sure. No problem." *More flies with honey. Remember that. More flies with honey.*

Not a chance had the detective caught me eavesdropping. I followed him out into the foyer of the inn.

"Thanks for the hospitality," Detective Goode said. "You doing all right?"

"Why wouldn't I be?" I asked. "I mean, yeah. I'm doing great. You let me know if you need anything, all right?"

"You're not planning on leaving town any time soon, are you?" His tone was stern.

So, the rumors are true. I'm a suspect. "Nope. Not any time soon. I'll be sure to let you know if I plan on it, Detective."

"Sure. OK. You keep well, Miss Smith."

"You too, Detective Goode."

He gave me a final look, one I couldn't place, then turned and walked out of the doors, letting them fall shut behind him.

❧ 10 ❧

That evening...

"I'm going to wring Billy's skinny little neck!" Lauren proclaimed, from behind the stovetop in the inn's kitchen. "I planned on doing waffle cupcakes the entire week, and now I can't do anything."

"Still no flour?" I asked. "I asked you Lauren. Are you sure you don't want me to check this out for you?"

"I doubt there's anything you can do,

Charlie, though I appreciate the offer. I mean, this isn't a case you can solve. It's a lack of supply." Lauren huffed and opened the oven door. She had a lasagna inside—one of her favorite dishes to make because she could load it with mushrooms from the "Shroom Shed" under the inn—Lauren's side project where she grew fresh mushrooms for the inn's meals.

The scents of melted cheese and bubbling sauce filled the kitchen.

We had everything set up for dinner—bread from The Bread Factory, fresh butter on the side—including the plates and cutlery. Lauren, Gamma, and I always ate after the guests and before the clean up, so it would be a while before I got to snack on Lauren's lasagna.

Thankfully, I had a distraction. The strange conversation that had taken place between Mandy and Detective Goode earlier played on my mind.

A funeral. Were they talking about Tina's funeral?

And how well had Tina and Mandy known each other?

I walked to the swinging kitchen doors with their porthole windows and peered out at the dining area.

Folks had already gathered at their tables in anticipation of their meals. Soft light from the chandeliers overhead gave the room a warm appearance for dinner.

Mandy sat at a table close to the window, its curtains now closed, sipping from a glass of water. I had gone out earlier to ensure the guests had the drinks they needed.

"Say, Laur," I said.

"Uh-huh?"

"What do you know about Mandy Gilmore?"

"Mandy... hmm. She's a regular old Gossip resident. Likes all the same things we do. Gossiping, food, and more gossiping." Lauren's temper flare over the flour had dissipated. She gave me one of her usual sweet smiles. "At least, she was a regular resident until she left."

"I heard about that. Any idea where she went when she left Gossip?"

"Rumor has it that she went off to the big

city. Dallas or Houston or somewhere to start her own business."

"What kind of business?" I asked.

"That I don't know, but it can't have been successful if she's back here so soon. She left like... a year ago, I think? I'm not sure of the timeline."

I fell silent, tightening my apron straps and considering it. Funny. A few years ago, the thought of apron straps and serving people who may or may not have been small town murderers would've been laughable.

"I heard her talking to Detective Goode earlier today. About a funeral of some sort."

"Oh?" Lauren asked. "Maybe she was talking about Tina's funeral."

"That's what I thought," I said. "But the way she was talking kind of made it sound like Tina would be attending the funeral too. Has anyone died recently that you know of? Someone popular in town?"

"Now, let me think." Lauren opened the oven door and checked her lasagna a second time. "I guess Mr. Tindell died a week ago. Old age. He was well-liked in the community, but I don't see why Tina or Mandy would've gone to the funeral."

"Interesting. Were Tina and Mandy friends?"

"Oh yeah, I'd say so. They went to high school together."

"With Josie," I said.

"Yeah. With Josie," Lauren replied. "They graduated the same year. I think Josie has an old yearbook lying around with their messages."

"So they were super close?"

"Not super close, no. They weren't best friends or anything, but they probably hung out? I don't know. They're older than me, so I'm not part of that crowd. I have my little family to spend time with." Lauren smiled, flattening her apron over her pregnant belly. "And the ghost in the basement."

Oh boy. Don't get sucked into that again. "OK. Thanks. I guess what I'm wondering is why Mandy would've visited Tina at the station because of Mr. Tindell's death."

"I don't know why. I don't think she would have but..."

"You don't know for sure. Thanks, Lauren. Sorry for pressuring you about this stuff."

"No way, Charlie. Whatever I can do to help."

She meant apart from me accusing her sister of course. Never anger a pregnant lady with murder accusations leveraged at her siblings. And never dispute the existence of ghosts in her basement. Or touch her recipe book.

There were a lot of "nevers" to take into account when it came to pregnant women. Not that I blamed Lauren. If I'd had what was effectively a parasite inside my body, feeding off everything I ate, I'd have been grumpy too.

Good thing that parasite would end up being a cute baby like Tyke.

"Lasagna's ready!" Lauren called, triumphantly, and removed the dishes from the oven. She set them on the countertop to cool, while I lined up plates.

We served a set menu based on what Lauren felt like serving every day, and it always went down a treat with the guests. But Lauren was careful to ask about allergies and dietary restrictions so that she considered everyone's needs.

"Are you going to be seeing your sister again soon?" I asked Lauren, as we dished up the slices of lasagna.

"Oh, some time, I imagine. We've been busy lately, her with what happened at the bakery and me here. But whenever we catch up, it's like we saw each other yesterday. That's how it is with siblings, isn't it?"

"Josie's at the bakery every day, right?"

"Sure is. She's a hard worker."

I made a mental note of it. Tomorrow morning, first thing, I'd be back at the bakery. Josie had lied to me, and I wanted answers.

The following morning...

I parked my grandmother's Mini-Cooper across the street from Josie's bakery, the sign on the front door now reading "OPEN" in bold lettering. A line of hungry patrons extended from within the bakery and down the sidewalk outside. The door had been wedged open so they could queue without obstruction.

Which was fascinating, really, because Tina's bakery wasn't doing as well.

While The Bread Factory was open down the street, it had suffered a serious lack of leadership. Mrs. Rogers, who had taken over from her daughter, was struggling to keep up, and there were less and less folks going to get their bread from the bakery as a result.

So, whether Josie had murdered Tina or not, she had directly benefited from her death.

I opened my case notes on my phone and went through them, adding information here or there.

Victim Name: *Tina Rogers.*

Victim Detail: *Baker. In legal trouble. Hired me to prove her innocence—accused of breaking into The Little Cake Shop owned by Josie Carlson.*

Cause of Death: *Murder. Weapon unknown. Potentially poisoning. Confirmation required.*

Suspects
Josie Carlson
Mandy Gilmore
Bridget Willows
Evidence

Glove embroidered specially for Tina found in Josie's bakery.

Brownie at crime scene.

Mary Moosmin? This is the one who made the gloves.

Links

Josie owned a bakery. Brownie was found next to the victim's hand.

Tina's glove was found in Josie's bakery. Tina claimed the glove wasn't hers.

Someone who visited Tina must've killed her.

Connection of Tina's "crime" to the murder?

Questions

Who baked the brownies?

Did the brownies contain poison?

What was the cause of death?

What did Officer Miller hear?

Who was the owner of the glove found in Josie's bakery if not Tina?

What was Mandy talking about to Detective Goode? What funeral?

Why did Mandy visit Tina?

Why did Josie lie about visiting Tina?

And why did Bridget Willows, head of the Gossip Sewing Club, visit Tina?

I had so many questions and so few answers. Frustrating.

"You won't find out anything else sitting around here." It was what my grandmother would've said to me. Gamma wanted to help with the case, and would, I'd bet my last waffle cupcake on it, but she had a kitten foster center to run and convert into a cat hotel. An ambitious endeavor.

I got out of the car and headed across the street to the bakery.

I squished past the folks queuing, ignoring the complaints about cutting the line, and moved to the front counter.

Josie's bakery helpers stood behind it, selling the glistening baked goods kept beneath the glass countertops, and making coffees to order.

"Excuse me," I said, waving at one of them. "Is Josie around?"

"She's in the office in the back," the woman said, barely glancing up from the coffee machine.

The office door was shut, but I moved around the side of the counter, ignoring a sharp look shot at me from a barista, and knocked on it.

Silence.

I knocked again.

"What?" Josie's voice snapped from inside. "I told you I don't want to be disturbed."

I opened the door and entered a cramped office. A filing cabinet, desk, computer, and two chairs were squished into the tiny carpeted space with a single window on the back wall. The blinds hanging over it needed replacing. While cramped, it wasn't dirty. Clearly, Josie cared about her business.

But were times tough? The decor in here was in need of updating. The computer was straight out of the age of the dinosaurs.

"What are you doing here?" Josie asked, glaring at me over the top of her computer screen. "I'm busy."

"I imagine you are," I said, with a quick smile. "It's packed out there. Business going great?"

"Yes," Josie replied, almost defiantly. "We were closed for a few days. People missed out on our food, so they want to get it while it's hot."

"Seems like you've picked up new clientele."

"And so?" Josie blew out a breath. "Look, I'm not interested in playing games or answering questions. I have things to do. So, if you would get out of—"

"You lied to me, Josie."

"Excuse me?"

"You lied to me." I grabbed the rickety chair in front of her desk and pulled it out, then sat down. *Channel Georgina. That's the only way.* "About Tina."

Josie's expression froze, as if she was afraid to change it. A mask she'd put up for fear of being exposed?

The more I looked at this case and all the evidence attached, the surer I became that Josie was involved. The murderer? Maybe. But there was a secret to be uncovered here.

"What about Tina?" Josie asked.

It was common, during interrogations, for the interrogator to become confrontational. Ask a question just like I had. Tell the suspect that they had lied. An innocent person would usually call out the confrontation. They would be outraged by the mere suggestion that they had done something wrong.

And the guilty person?

They would deflect. Or try to seem innocent. They wouldn't point out the confrontation.

I let Josie's question hang in the air while I considered her.

"What about Tina?" she repeated.

No denial of the lie.

"You told me that the last time you saw Tina was a few days ago. But I have it on good authority that you saw her on the morning of her death. That you visited her at the police station."

Josie whitened, but didn't talk.

"Why didn't you tell me you saw her that morning?"

"Well, uh. I didn't realize I'd seen her that morning." Josie forced a laugh. "I don't keep track of who I talk to and when. As you can tell, I'm, uh, I'm a very busy woman."

And I'm Santa Claus. "Right. But wouldn't

you say that when you last saw Tina would be a memorable event? Not only had she been murdered but she was the one who broke into your bakery, right?"

"I don't know," Josie said, squeaking around in her office chair. "I'm waiting for the cops to tell me whether that's the case or not."

"OK. But you would remember, right?"

"Look, I'm a busy woman," Josie repeated, roughly this time. "And I'm sure Lauren wouldn't appreciate you harassing me like this. I thought you were supposed to be helping figure out who broke into my bakery? What's this got to do with whether Tina did it or not?"

"Everything," I said, rising from my seat. "What did you and Tina talk about at the police station?"

"I don't remember."

"Seriously. You don't remember?"

"No, I don't remember," Josie said. "It can't have been important."

"You don't remember talking to the woman who allegedly broke into your bakery, vandalized it, and stole from you?"

"No, I don't remember."

I stared at Josie for a hot minute, but she didn't give me anything else.

"I have work to do." Josie tried for her usual bossy attitude, but it fell flat.

"Right." I nodded. "Enjoy your work." And then I left.

I wasn't going to get anything else out of Josie today, and I had other leads to follow. Like where the brownies had come from, and why Officer Miller had let them get to Tina in the holding cell.

12

The Gossip Police Station was a single story building, the flag flying on the front lawn. It was pretty as a peach on the outside. White, with glass doors, and a view of the reception area inside, one would've been excused for thinking it was a nice place to be.

I parked my grandmother's Mini-Cooper in a space out front then exited into the morning sunshine. My goal was simple.

Get in there, schmooze with Officer Miller to get him to tell me who had given

Tina the brownies, and avoid Detective Goode's notice at all costs.

I couldn't afford to get on his bad side on purpose.

The whole "don't leave town" spiel he'd given me had made it clear that I was a suspect, and though I didn't necessarily have a cover to blow anymore because I was retired, I still didn't want to draw attention to the inn in a negative light. Or my grandmother.

A few people passed by on the sidewalk, recognized me, and greeted.

I loved that about small towns. There was such a sense of community. A welcome and feeling of safety, even when there was a murderer on the loose.

I walked up the front steps and headed into the reception area. The woman behind the worn wood desk looked up from her computer, dark half-moons under her eyes. She was washed out and pale, hair gray and frizzy. "Hello honey," she said. "What can I help you with?"

"I'm looking for Officer Miller. Is he around?"

"Sure, he is. I'll call him out here for you." The receptionist picked up the receiver on her desk phone and punched a few buttons. "Greg? Yeah, I've got a young lady here to see you. Sure. One sec." She covered the receiver. "What's your name, honey?"

"Charlotte Smith."

"It's Charlotte Smith. Would you—? Oh, great. OK." She hung up the receiver. "He'll be out in a sec."

"Thank you." I backed away from the receptionist, leaving her to her work, and peered out of the glass front doors. Bathed in sunlight, a perfect Gossip day, with people going about their business in the streets with trees emerging from beds in the concrete, wrought iron benches and lampposts.

Quiet.

Nothing like my life had been once upon a time. The itch to keep busy would always be there, to be useful.

"Miss Smith?" Officer Miller stopped next to me. "Is there a problem? Something you'd like to report?"

There's always a problem to fix in this town.

"Would you mind stepping outdoors with me, please, Officer? I had a few questions. I'm kind of worried about something." I put up my brightest smile and fluffed my short blonde hair—finally back to its natural color after an undercover stint last year.

"Sure," he said, cheeks pinking. "Sure, yeah. Sure. I can do that."

Another trick from my grandmother. Never be afraid to use your feminine wiles.

We stepped out of the police station, and I led the way—down the steps, off to one side, onto the grass near the cute signboard bearing the name of the station.

"What's the problem, Miss Smith?" Officer Miller—in his early forties with a few gray hairs, a full head of dark hair, and a nose that looked as if it had been broken. He had a scar above his left eyebrow that was white against his tan skin.

"I had a few questions about what happened to Tina Rogers."

"Oh," he said. "That. Man, I've been hearing *a lot* about that lately. A lot more than I'd like to hear."

"Did you get in any trouble for what happened?"

Officer Miller shrugged.

"Look, I know this might be a little out there, but I need some help, Officer. You see, before she died, Tina wanted me to figure out what happened at The Little Cake Shop. She told me that she was innocent and that someone had set her up." Honesty felt like the best policy in this instance. Officer Miller was a cop—he could smell manure a mile off, the verbal kind only I hoped.

"OK?"

"I know that there were people who visited her that morning, and I sure don't expect you to tell me who they were, but the brownies..."

Officer Miller didn't say anything. He ran a hand over his forehead, fingers feeling the scar.

"How did they get into the holding cell?"

"I'm not allowed to talk about murder cases," Officer Miller said. "Or investigations."

"I know," I said. "But I'm not asking because of the murder case. I'm doing private research into what happened at The Little Cake Shop." Officer Miller would have every right to tell me to get lost, right about now. "And it's for Tina's mother. Mrs. Rogers. You know her, don't you?"

Officer Miller nodded. "Mrs. Rogers is friends with my mom."

"Right. OK. Look, it's the only question I have, and I promise I won't bother you with anything else."

Officer Miller's feeling of the scar intensified. "I wish I could tell you," he said. "I really do, but, yeah. I don't know how the brownies got in there to her. I made everybody sign in, and I searched them."

I cast my mind back to how Miller had searched me. A quick pat down that hadn't exactly been thorough. It would've been easy to smuggle in a small package, hidden under my shirt, pressed flat, even taped to my torso.

"So, you have no idea who brought them in for her either?" I asked.

The brownies might not have been poisoned, but they were an important part of the investigation. The fact was, someone wanted to give Tina baked goods, or Tina had asked for them, and with the bakery information flying around, it had to be relevant.

"No. I don't know. Sorry." Officer Miller glanced at the station. "I should go."

"Thanks, Officer." I offered him a grateful smile. "I appreciate the help."

"Sure," he replied. "But a word of advice, Miss Smith?"

"Yeah?"

"Stay out of Detective Goode's way. He came down from Dallas, and he means business." He loped off toward the police station, leaving me with that sour food for thought.

❧ 13 ❧

"Y ou know what this means." Gamma was seated on our rendezvous bench under the trees in front of the inn, her hands folded neatly in her lap. She had chosen a pair of ironed jeans and a silk blouse today, complete with a string of pearls.

"I hope I do," I said.

Gamma gave me one of her trademark sneaky smiles. "Meet me at the spot in five minutes. I'll approach from inside the inn, you take the outside."

"Copy."

Gamma left me sitting on the bench with

a few minutes of down time to consider our next steps. The "spot" as she'd called it, was our meeting point at the back of the inn. No one but my grandmother, me, and one other agent who wouldn't out us, knew about what was underneath the inn.

The Shroom Shed.

And my grandmother's super secret armory, stocked with every piece of equipment the budding and experienced spy might need. We'd be using it today to get more information about one suspect in particular.

Josie Carlson.

She had lied to me, avoided my questions, and I was becoming increasingly convinced that she had been the one who'd given Tina the brownies at the police station.

Five minutes later, I rounded the inn, using the neat gravel pathway that ran alongside it, and met my grandmother outside the basement doors. She held the ornate key to the door, waiting for me, impatiently.

"By all means, Charlotte, take your time. It's not as if we have a murderer to catch."

I flashed her a grin. "I've missed you, Georgina. You've been busy."

"Yes, well, getting the cat hotel set up has been nothing short of hot and fiery." She bent and unlocked the ornate lock on the basement doors—they were wooden, old, but decorated in luminous paintings of mushrooms.

We entered the dark, dampness underneath the inn, and Gamma closed the doors behind us. Quickly, we wound past the darkened Shroom Shed, and toward the doorway separating this section of the basement from the armory.

My grandmother used retina identification, her thumb print, and a key, to grant us access.

The lights in her armory flicked on, revealing rows of shelving, stocked with weaponry, ammo, and devices, all organized meticulously. A clap of my grandmother's hands opened the hidden weapon compartments on the wall. They emerged with a pneumatic hiss. The armor stands, two for women, one for men, held black clothing made from material that was breathable, fire resistant, and bullet resistant.

I stopped inside the door, inhaling the scent of this place—a hint of gunpowder, but mostly that "new device" smell. My grandmother's armory never ceased to amaze me.

"All right," Gamma said, and headed over to her touchscreen desk at the front of the room, closest to the door. "Target name is Josie Carlson." She took her seat on the ergonomic leather chair and tapped on her desktop, bringing up information with ease. "Let's see, what do we have here?"

"We're not going in hot, are we?" I asked. "I doubt we'll need weapons for reconnaissance."

"Oh, Charlotte, you'd swear this was your first time running Intel with me."

I rolled my eyes at her, but she ignored me like I was a teenager. Not far off with the eye-rolling.

"Josie Carlson," my grandmother said, bringing up the information she had on file. My grandmother kept a file on everyone in

Gossip, new and old, and was religious about updating her database.

When I'd first arrived in Gossip, I hadn't understood why she would need this, other than because she was bored of the quiet life after years as the NSIB's top spy. But now, I got it. It was good to be prepared, especially when there was danger around every corner.

And it helped Gamma keep control of the situation with Jessie Belle-Blue and her competing guesthouse.

"Her usual movements include arriving at The Little Cake Shop at 07:00 a.m., lunch at the Hungry Steer between 12:00 p.m. and 01:00 p.m., arrival at home at 06:30 p.m.. She goes to church every Sunday, and she has a book club meeting on Thursdays."

"Anything about the Sewing Club in there?" I asked.

"No. She doesn't attend," Gamma replied.

"And was she friends with Tina Rogers?"

"I don't have that noted down," Gamma replied. "My list of information isn't inexhaustible. Otherwise, you wouldn't have to go out and ask people questions, would you, Charlotte?"

"Fair."

Gamma sent Josie's home address to her phone then dismissed her information and rose from her chair. "We will need something special this evening. Listening devices that can pick up on what's going on inside Josie's house, attuned to conversation. That way, we won't have to listen to the blaring of a TV while we're there."

"What do you suggest?"

Gamma tapped her nose then walked to a central glass case between the shelves. She hit a button on the side of it, and the glass slid into the white stand, revealing a black "bug" and a small remote next to it.

"What's this?" I asked.

Gamma removed both items and held up the smaller object. "This," she said, "is my fly on the wall. FlyBoy Drone. Brand new technology from one of my contacts at the Pentagon. Watch this." She lifted the remote and hit a button.

The tiny bug whirred to life and flew from her hand, hovering in front of my face.

"Silent and stealthy, it can be flown through the crack of a door or a keyhole to listen in on top secret conversations." She grinned. "It attunes to a set earpiece to relay information in crystal clear quality."

"Wow."

Gamma guided the drone back to her palm with a few taps of buttons on the remote. "Wow, indeed. If Josie has anything to hide, we're about to find out what it is."

❧

WE TOOK MY GRANDMOTHER'S NEWLY commissioned black SUV—a gift from an old spy buddy who had owed her a favor—out at 09:00 p.m., after the dinner service and the dishes were done. Everyone in Gossip knew what my grandmother's Mini-Cooper looked like, so driving that on a top secret mission was out of the question.

Gamma parked the SUV down the road from Josie's house on Trickle Down Avenue before getting out of the car in the fading light. She flew the FlyBoy Drone toward the house, guiding it with a connected VR headset, and flew it in through the keyhole.

"Can I see the video feed?" I asked, once my grandmother was back inside the SUV.

"I can link that up to this." Gamma tapped the screen attached to her dashboard. The car had come fully equipped with everything needed for high-tech surveillance. My grandmother fiddled with some settings and the image appeared on the screen.

The FlyBoy Drone had settled on the wall in the living room which was HD quality on the screen.

"Man, this is good," I murmured.

"Only the best. One shouldn't be saddled with terrible surveillance equipment. It only makes the job more difficult," Gamma said, sagely.

"Oh! There she is."

Josie strode into view, fiddling on her cell phone, and her expression wasn't happy. She plopped down on the sofa and switched on the TV. I fully expected a blast of ear-splitting noise, but the noise from the TV barely registered.

"That's impressive."

"I told you," Gamma said. "Cancels out all noise except for conversation. To the best of it's abilities." She moved the fly a little on the wall to get a better view of Josie.

"What happens when someone spots it and decides to use bug spray or a swatter?"

"Evasive maneuvers," Gamma replied. "This bug goes incredibly fast. If somebody hits it out of the air, it will be the pilot's fault."

"Remind me to never try flying this thing."

"No reminder required. I simply won't allow you to."

That was probably for the best.

Josie's phone rang, and she lifted it to her ear. Gamma and I quieted.

"Yeah? Oh, hey. Yeah, no, everything's fine. I told you, you don't need to worry about me." Josie paused and listened to what the person on the other end of the phone was saying. "Seriously? Ugh. Why would you even bring that up again? I am so not... No. Lauren. Stop it."

"It's Lauren," I said. "A sisterly phone call."

"She's probably concerned about Josie because of Tina's death. Lauren's not oblivious to how suspicious her sister looks."

"Look, I don't want to talk about it. My heart is not broken. My life is not over. I only care about the bakery now, so it's fine." Another long silence. "No, I'm not going to tell you who it is. Yeah. OK. Love you too. See you on Sunday for dinner. Do *not* bring that husband of yours, OK? No. I don't care. Listen, I've made it clear how I feel about him so... OK, OK. Bye." Josie hung up, shaking her head, and turned back to the TV.

"Heart broken?" I asked. "Josie?"

"Maybe over Tina. Maybe some relationship issue. Who knows. Not what we wanted. We need her talking openly about Tina to someone. Let's hope that happens."

But I didn't hold out any hope. Even with the fantastic drone at our disposal, we couldn't force Josie to say the things we needed her to say.

❧ 14 ❧

The following morning...

Our evening reconnaissance mission hadn't gotten us much closer to figuring out anything about Tina's death. Josie had watched TV for an hour without talking to anyone else on the phone then had gone to bed.

We'd parked in front of her house for another few hours then gave it up and returned to the Gossip Inn.

I had to face facts. The Josie portion of this investigation wasn't going anywhere. And I had other suspects I needed to consider. Like Mandy Gilmore and this head of the Gossip Sewing Club lady.

Breakfast time came, and after another round of complaints about the lack of flour and cupcakes from Lauren, I exited into the dining room to make my rounds with a pot of coffee. The space was already packed with guests, including my target.

Mandy Gilmore sat at a glossy, wooden table in front of the window, her chin resting on her palm as she stared out at the inn's sweeping front lawn. Pensive? Guilty? Upset? She wore black today, which said something.

I wasn't sure what it said, but it said *something*.

I made my rounds through the dining area, smiling at the guests, offering coffee, answering questions about what was for break-fast, and fielding complaints. Opal, the gossipy guest from a couple of days back, had a lot to say about the lack of cupcake offer-ings. Heaven forbid, Lauren heard her.

Finally, I wound up at Mandy's table.

"Coffee?" I asked, sweetly.

"Yeah, that would be great, thank you." She tossed her dark hair, offering a wan smile. "You're the one who came to my room the other day, right?"

"That's right," I said, filling her mug. "I'm here every day. If you ever need anything, just let me know."

"Thank you. I will." She wasn't as sniffy today, and she didn't look down her upturned nose at me. "I'm... listen, I think I was a little rude to you when Detective Goode was here. I wanted to apologize."

"There's no need."

"There is. I'm sorry for being rude. I've been a bit upset, that's all."

"Because of Tina?" I asked, pretending that it was a wild guess. "I noticed you were wearing black, and I thought it was probably about her. I know Tina had a lot of friends."

"She did. She was a lovely person. You know, she built her bakery from the ground up. I always felt like... she was an inspiration.

Not like that wretched—ugh, listen to me. I shouldn't say."

"Please, go ahead. Sometimes, it's good to get this kind of stuff out." That was my excuse and I was sticking to it. I'd gotten better at small talk, but I wasn't a pro by any means.

Mandy gave me a look like she didn't know quite what to make of what I'd said, but shook it off a second later. "Josie. I'm not a big fan of Josie. I know she gave Tina trouble lately, that's all. Tina complained to me about her because she was arrested on these ridiculous breaking and entering charges. Everybody knows that The Bread Factory does better than The Little Cake Shop. Tina would have no reason to vandalize Josie's place."

"I heard that too," I lied. "That's crazy."

"All of this is crazy," Mandy said, and took a sip of her coffee. "Sometimes, I think the whole town is crazy."

"Something in the water."

Mandy offered the barest of giggles. "Exactly."

"It's so sad about what happened to Tina," I said. "Really puzzling too." Mandy hadn't been in Gossip for a year, according to my information from Lauren. She wouldn't know that I liked to poke my nose in murder investigations. Hopefully, that worked in my favor.

"It's terrible."

"I wonder who did it," I said.

Mandy shook her head, ruefully. "I wonder too." More head shaking. "But... oh no, I shouldn't say."

I encouraged her to continue by slipping into the empty seat opposite her and placing the coffee pot on the table.

"Tina recently broke up with a guy," Mandy said, after another sip of coffee. "A guy she was desperately in love with, but it didn't work out."

"Why?"

"Because the guy was too possessive. She loved him, but his behavior was out there. He proposed to her after they had only been dating for two months, and she said no. She was upset, but he was even more upset. He had a temper, Brick."

"Brick? The guy's name is Brick?"

"Uh-huh, yeah. Brick Jonas."

"That's quite the name," I said.

Mandy shifted to the edge of her seat. "I'll tell you a secret. The worst kept one in Gossip. Brick was as dumb as his name. And had the tendency to fly off the handle too. Temper, like I said. I never understood what Tina saw in him."

"Do you think...?"

"Oh yeah. If anyone wanted to get rid of her, it was Brick."

"You think so?"

"Definitely." Mandy shook her head. "It's terrible. That man should be behind bars."

The kitchen doors opened, and Lauren waved at me from them. It was time to start serving the guests. "It was nice chatting," I said, then got up and excused myself.

Mandy was still a suspect, but I'd found another name to add to my list.

Brick Jonas.

❦ 15 ❦

"Intriguing," Gamma said. "Very intriguing." She held my phone with my updated notes and scrolled through them. "Brick Jonas. I know that boy. Slowest one of his bunch during high school, so the rumors say."

We sat in the library this time. Well, Gamma sat in one of the cushy green velvet armchairs while I dusted the spines of the books, questions sprouting lightning fast. Where was Brick? Would he have been able to murder Tina? His name hadn't been on the visitor's list.

Was there a way that Brick might've gotten into the police station to see Tina without Officer Miller knowing?

"What can you tell me about Brick?" I asked, stopping and gesturing at my grand-mother with the feather duster.

Sunlight, my ginger cat, had positioned himself on the arm of another of the chairs. He meowed at me.

"What?" I asked. "It's a valid question." Once upon a time, I would've thought myself crazy for talking to cats. Now, it was an everyday occurrence. And not just in the cutesy "baby voice" way.

Another meow from Sunlight.

"Don't argue with me."

"Are you quite finished, Charlotte?" Gamma asked.

"Yeah, yeah," I said.

"Brick Jonas is in his late thirties. He is as thick as a... well, a brick."

"The joke has already been made."

Georgina tapped her fingertips on the arms of her chair. "It's news to me that he was dating Tina. This must be a new development."

"Two months in the making, apparently. He tried to propose."

"Goodness, I *have* been slacking. I must update my database," Gamma said. "I've been so busy with the kitten foster center..." She clicked her tongue. "No excuses."

"Does Brick have contacts at the police station?" I asked.

"Contacts?"

"Yes."

"Charlotte, everyone in Gossip has contacts with everyone else. It's highly likely he was friendly with someone at the police station." Gamma paused, her gaze shrewd. "You're wondering if he managed to get in and see her without being written down on the visitor's list."

"Yes."

"Perhaps. I can check with my grapevine. There's a world where that could happen. The Gossip Police Station isn't usually that busy. The officers service the entire county and the two smaller towns close by, so it's possible."

"That makes him a valid suspect," I said. "I'll need to talk to him. Soon."

"Any other avenues to investigate? Surely, you don't plan on investigating just the one."

I dropped into the armchair where Sunlight had positioned himself, and he climbed into my lap, purring. I stroked his furry head, considering what my next steps would be. "The glove," I said, at last. "When I spoke to Tina on the phone, she told me the glove wasn't hers. That was the reason she believed she could make the police pay, her words not mine, for having arrested her. So who does the glove belong to?"

"Sounds like you need to talk to the glove maker. Mary Moosmin. Or one better, the head of the Gossip Sewing Club. She was on the suspect list, correct?"

"That's right." I paused my stroking and Sunlight let out a *prrt* as a complaint. I resumed petting him. "Brick Jonas, the Gossip Sewing Club, and Josie. My three main avenues. I didn't squeeze much information out of Mandy, so I'll have to talk to her again about seeing Tina on the morning of her death. I'll phrase the question innocently. Say I'm trying to prove Tina's innocence in the theft case at The Little Cake Shop. Mandy had a negative opinion of Josie, so it should work."

"Capital idea," Gamma said. "That's settled. Oh, Charlotte, I've been meaning to talk to you about Mr. Grote's cat."

"The Houdini of cats." The feline that had escaped and gotten into flour in the pantry, though we weren't sure how yet. "What about him?"

"The cat is fine, secured in the kitten foster center, soon to be hotel," Gamma replied. "The trouble is, I can't figure out how the little blighter escaped. The secret passages in the center have been closed off."

The Gossip Inn had many secret passages and areas, including one in this very library.

"I'm puzzled about it too. But we don't know every passage, Georgina. There's got to be some way the cat escaped."

Gamma sighed. "Yes, I'll look into it." She got out of her chair and passed me by, pausing at the library door. "Call me if you have any plans to go adventuring, Charlotte."

"I will. You can bet I will." I needed my grandmother's help and her full arsenal of spy gear if I was going to solve the case.

My grandmother left me to consider my path forward. I would talk to Brick, I would head on down to the Gossip Sewing Club headquarters, wherever they were, and I would finally work out what had happened to Tina Rogers.

And why. That was what bothered me the most about this case. I couldn't see a good reason why Tina had been murdered. What was the motive?

❄ 16 ❆

I let myself out of the library after dusting the spines of a few more books while Sunlight played around the tables, darting to and fro. He had a serious case of the zoomies, but I didn't mind. Sunlight's antics put me in a good mood.

It was just past 10:00 a.m., and I'd be due to help Lauren start the lunch service soon. Time was of the essence—I needed to get out of the inn and go see Brick Jonas as soon as possible.

Hurriedly, I stored the feather duster in the hall closet then started up the stairs to go get changed. I paused on the second floor landing, my eyes widening.

The inn's wooden halls with their trinket nooks were empty between meals. The guests didn't mingle unless they had arrived at the inn together, and this week's guests certainly hadn't.

Then what, oh what is she *doing?*

Opal, the woman who had been arguing with Mandy at the start of the week, stood frozen in the hall, her back to me, her ear pressed against a door.

It hit me fast. A jolt out of the blue. That was the Rose Room! Mandy was staying there.

So, what on earth was Opal doing with her ear pressed to the door? Eavesdropping, obviously, but why?

I considered confronting her, but that would ruin the moment. It was more interesting to observe.

Quietly, I checked my watch then wriggled my nose back and forth. I couldn't hang around much longer, anyway. I needed to get out, fast.

Opal pushed away from the door just as I

was about to head up to my room. She spotted me, turning the approximate color of a beet.

"I-I was just—I—"

"No need to explain," I said, and started up the stairs. I didn't have time to waste, and then there was the fact that I had places to be. Opal wouldn't tell me the truth about why she'd been spying on Mandy anyway.

Regardless, I made a mental note of it. If Opal was spying on Mandy, she might be a person of interest. Or it was completely unrelated and more of the usual crazy Gossip behavior. Only time, and thorough investigation, would tell.

BRICK JONAS' FAVORITE HAUNT WAS THE park, according to my grandmother's grapevine. I headed over as fast as I could without breaking any speed limits, and parked under an oak tree, its leaves occasionally shaken by the wind.

Gossip's park was vast and filled with green grass, trees, and a central pond where folks sat and chatted at their leisure. People walked their dogs, keeping them strictly on their leads as per park rules, and others pushed their children on a set of swings.

The usual small town atmosphere—pleasant and bubbling with an undertone of murder.

Maybe that was just my take on things.

I entered the park, tucking my hands into my pockets, and strolled along. Gamma had gotten me a picture of my mark from her database, whilst frantically updating it to include Brick's dating history, and I kept an eye out for him.

In his thirties, blonde hair with a widow's peak, nose too small for the face, large, expressive lips. The picture I'd seen of him made it look as if he'd been pieced together by an uninspired painter. Or a sculptor who'd inhaled too many paint fumes. Or wait, no, it would be the painter who—

My mind chatter cut off.

The mark was in my sights.

Brick wore a loose tank top, his muscular arms exposed, and his large hands grasping a football. "Go long!" he shouted at a man who was already going long. "Longer!" He had a voice like a foghorn.

Maybe I was being hard on the guy, but he didn't give off a great first vibe.

Brick tossed the football at his friend, and the other guy caught it with a whoop of excitement.

"Yeah!" Brick yelled. "Throw it back, Todd. Throw it back."

Todd proceeded to do as he was told. The football swooped through the air and bounced off my head. Todd needed to work on his aim.

"Ouch." I held my head, even though it hadn't hurt that much. It was time to play the damsel in distress card. "Ouch. Wow."

"Oh man, are you OK?" Brick ran over to me, his dark eyes filled with concern. This guy was tall. He was the type of guy who was so tall it was intimidating. The type who would find it easy to overpower and kill a person.

"Ow. Man, that kills." I held my head, glancing up at him from under my brow.

"Todd, you dumbo! You hurt the lady."

"Aw, man!" Todd ran over too. "I'm sorry. Are you OK?"

"Of course, she's not OK. Look at her. She's practically crying." Brick whacked his friend on his burly chest. "Help me get her over to a bench."

"I'm fine," I said. "Really."

"See, she's OK." Todd gave a grin that was the opposite of enigmatic. He jogged off again, calling to his other friends and leaving me with my mark.

Perfect.

This couldn't have gone better. Minus the ball to my head, but whatever.

"You sure you're OK?" Brick asked.

"I'm OK," I said. "Thanks. I'm Charlotte, by the way." I straightened, sticking out a hand and hamming it up with a wince.

"Brick. Brick Jonas," he replied, squeezing my hand so hard he crushed my fingers together. "Nice to meet you too."

"Wait," I said. "Wait a second. You're Brick?" *Here goes nothing.*

"You know me?"

"I know of you," I said. "My friend Tina told me all about you. Tina Rogers?"

Brick's concern fell from his face like scales from the eyes. "Oh."

"Sorry, did I say something wrong? Tina told me so much about you. You're her boyfriend, right?"

He folded his muscly arms. "Nope."

"Wait, what? You're not? I'm so sorry. I thought... she told me..."

"We broke up."

"Oh, man, I'm so sorry. How did I manage to put my foot in my mouth about this?" I slapped my head and remembered to act like it had hurt. "Ouchies. Sorry about bringing up Tina. I haven't spoken to her in a while," I said, leading him in the conversation. This *had* to work. "I'll have to call her later to catch up."

"You can't."

"I can't?"

"No, you can't," he said. "She's dead."

I sucked in a gasp. "She's... no. What? How?"

"Somebody killed her." He pronounced "killed" as "kilt."

My jaw dropped, and I gaped at him. "You can't be serious."

"Yeah. She's dead." And that was it. Not even an attempt to act like he was upset about it.

"I'm sorry," I said. "That's terrible."

He shrugged. "You sure you're OK, lady?"

"I'm fine."

"Good. I gotta go." And off he ran.

That was like getting blood from a stone. The man was as his name proclaimed, but that meant I couldn't get much without sustained prodding. Regardless, Brick hadn't shed a tear for Tina.

And I didn't have any useful information from this conversation.

On to the next lead.

❧ 17 ❧

The headquarters of the Gossip Sewing Club weren't far away, so I opted to leave my grandmother's Mini-Cooper in the shade of the old oak at the park and take a leisurely stroll through Gossip. I needed time to drag my heels and sulk over my lack of progress.

I wasn't a private investigator or an ex-cop. I was good at wringing people for information —assuming they had enough personality and intelligence to be wrung—and finding hidden Intel. But actually following leads?

I'd helped solve a couple cases, but this had grown complex.

Three people had visited Tina. She'd died in what was essentially a locked cage. And I had no idea about the cause of death.

Keep chipping away at it. Mrs. Rogers is counting on you.

I turned into Baker Avenue before noon, checking my phone in case Lauren called to ask me where I was. I'd texted my grandmother and asked her to fill in for me in the kitchen while I finished following a final lead. Hopefully, Lauren wouldn't need my help soon.

My feet carried me past The Little Cake Shop, doing a roaring trade thanks to The Bread Factory's lack of offerings, and past the entrance to an alleyway a few doors down.

A shout tore through the air.

I spun on my heel, searching for the source of the disturbance. The calm that I'd been trained into descended.

There!

A hooded figure had a woman pressed up

against the wall. The glint of a knife in the figure's hand.

"Hey!" I yelled. "Don't move."

Adrenaline kicked in, and I launched into action, darting toward the hooded attacker. They released their victim, instantly, and took off for the opposite end of the alleyway. There wasn't a fence to block their passage.

I pumped my arms back and forth, regretting the extra cupcakes I'd eaten at the inn over the past couple of months. But the person was too fast. They escaped into the busy street opposite.

I exited onto the sidewalk, nearly slamming into an old woman with her Chihuahua in her purse.

"Watch it," she yelped.

"Sorry." I skidded to a halt, casting wild looks left and right, but the figure was gone. They had disappeared, either into one of the stores on the street or down another alleyway. "Did you see—?

But the woman I'd bumped into had already headed off, huffing under her breath about rude young ladies.

"Darn."

A soft cry from the alleyway drew my attention. Of course! The woman who had been attacked.

I hurried back to her, slowing once I was a few feet away.

It was Josie. She sat against the brick wall of the alleyway, sucking in breaths, her hand pressed to her pale forehead.

"Are you OK?" I asked. "Were you hurt? Did they stab you?" I brought my cell phone out of my pocket to call 911.

Josie shook her head. "I'm not hurt."

"I'll call the cops."

"It's fine," Josie said. "You don't have to do that."

I stared at her as if she'd sprouted a set of horns. "You're kidding, right? Josie, did you hit your head? That person just attacked you."

"Yeah." Josie squeezed her eyes shut and took deep breaths. "I'm aware of that, but I'm fine. I just need a minute to calm down, that's all. It's no big deal."

"No big deal." Why didn't Josie want me to call the police? She'd been attacked, for heaven's sake. This wasn't normal. "Josie, you need to report this. If there's a serial mugger on the loose—"

"I told you, I don't want to," Josie snapped. "Help me up."

I stuck out my hand and pulled her up. "Did you know that person?"

"Don't be dumb," Josie snapped. "How would I know them? They were wearing a hoodie and a face mask thing. Sometimes, I wonder what that Georgina sees in you. Why employ a woman who is so clueless?"

Every inch of me wanted to bite back at her, but that wouldn't help the case. "How did this happen, Josie? How did the attacker sneak up on you?"

"I don't know," Josie said.

"What were you doing out here?"

"None of your business!" Josie marched off, disappearing into the street.

I stared at the spot where she'd been, trying to piece things together. Josie had been out in this alleyway alone, doing what? The person who had attacked her had run instead of confronting me. Did that mean that the attacker was the murderer? And if that was the case, was Josie innocent?

Then why the weird behavior? Why lie?

I shook my head and set off, moving back onto the sidewalk on Baker Avenue. I would get to the bottom of Josie's behavior, but first, I had a glove maker to question.

❧ 18 ❧

Not technically a glove maker. The head of the Gossip Sewing Club sat in a fusty armchair covered in floral print, her ankles crossed, and her hands in her lap. She wore her gray hair in curls, tight against her scalp, and had wrinkles that'd come from smiling.

First impressions should tell me that she was a harmless old lady who meant well. But I had a grandmother who could incapacitate a grown man with a debilitating nerve pinch maneuver using all of three fingers.

Experience said, "Don't trust the book's

cover or the book." Unless it was written by Agatha Christie.

"Are you sure you don't want something to drink, dear?" Mrs. Willows asked.

Bridget Willows, the third suspect on my list and the last to visit Tina before her death, ran the Gossip Sewing Club from her home, and, according to my grandmother, the community center, where the women met twice a week.

"Dear?"

Gosh, me getting lost in my thoughts again. "No, I'm good thank you, Mrs. Willows. I appreciate you taking the time to talk to me today. I know it might be strange that I'm asking questions about Tina."

"It's not strange," Mrs. Willows said, patting her curls. "I'm close with Tina's mother, Ursula, and she mentioned that you might stop by. I'm more than happy to help, whether it's with the case of Tina's missing glove, the break-in at The Little Cake Shop or Tina's..." Mrs. Willows paused to clear her throat, apparently choking up. "Tina's passing."

I gave a sympathetic nod. *Play the part.*

"Thank you for offering to help," I said. "And for inviting me into your home."

The living room was small, but neatly kept, even if the furniture was outdated. The house itself was a single story tucked between two others of its kind, with a miniscule front yard and no porch to speak of.

So, Mrs. Willows wasn't exactly rich, but she didn't stand to gain anything from Tina's death. Unless it came out that Tina had left her The Bread Factory. Unlikely, given that Ursula was now running the place. *Into the ground.*

"What was your relationship with Tina, Mrs. Willows?"

"I was her mentor," she said, proudly. "Tina was a part of the Gossip Sewing Club and the Young Ladies Business Club. I run both of them, and for a select few young ladies who show significant promise, I offer personal mentoring."

"What type of mentoring?"

"How to navigate society and the business world. How to become better at being a member of the community. Networking. Business training and so on. The young ladies are selected according to their business acumen, so it's a small group."

"And Tina was a part of that group."

"Yes."

Mrs. Willows mentored people from her tiny home? "Do you run a business yourself?" I asked, trying to find a nice way to ask the question.

"I used to. And I was a large part of my husband's success before his passing."

"What does your mentoring include?" It might not be relevant to Tina's death, but I was curious about the dichotomy. Of course, business success didn't equal mansions and cars, necessarily, but you wouldn't get weight loss tips from somebody who ate junk food and nothing else.

You can talk, cupcake queen.

"We go away to conferences, and I give them exclusive access to my business course, as well as other networking opportunities."

"Cool," I said, smiling. "Very nice. This might be a touchy subject Mrs. Willows, but may I ask what you and Tina discussed on the morning... it happened?"

"Yes, of course. I visited her to tell her that she had my faith, and that I would be praying for her, and that I had managed to put off the business trip we had been planning and move it to another date."

A straight answer. It was refreshing after Josie's question dodging.

"How did Tina seem to you when you talked to her?"

"She was upset. As she rightfully should have been given the circumstances. She was angry that she was behind bars."

"That's all she was upset about? There was nothing else bothering her?"

"There might have been," Mrs. Willows said. "But I didn't ask. We focused mainly on business topics and comfort for her unfortunate situation."

I nodded. "OK, got it. What about brownies? Did you bring Tina brownies?"

"No, I didn't." Bridget seemed confused. "Brownies?"

"Did she have any brownies on her while

you were there?"

"Not that I could see."

Dead end. "And, about Tina's glove..."

"Oh, dear, the glove that caused this mess? Yes, Tina was aggravated about that. She mentioned a meeting with you later and that she'd be talking to you about it, but nothing else."

"Were those gloves the only one of their kind? The embroidery, I mean."

"As far as I'm aware, yes. But you'll have to talk to Mary about that," Mrs. Willows said. "She's the one who made them, and I'm afraid I didn't know Tina that well back then. All I know is that it was a private commissioned pair of gloves."

That's not odd. "You're talking about Mary Moosmin, yes?"

"That's correct."

"Do you have her contact details? I'd like to talk to her too." I had a feeling that Mary would either cast light on the investigation or be of no help. I needed to find out which.

"I'm afraid I can't do that." Mrs. Willows pulled a face. "Mary's on vacation. She should be back sometime soon, but I never know with her. She lets the wind take her where it will most days."

If only we could all be so uninhibited. "That's all I need for now, Mrs. Willows. Thank you."

❧ 19 ❧

By the time I arrived back at the inn, the lunch service was over, clean up had been completed, and Lauren and Gamma had gone off for a drive in Lauren's little car. That was fine, I needed time to think, and Lauren, bless her heart, had left me lunch under a cover on the kitchen table.

I swept the cover off to reveal a fresh summer salad topped with roasted beets and a chicken breast with a honey-mustard glaze. I poured myself a glass of water then settled down to my meal.

"Oh man, this is good."

The chicken was succulent, the dressing tangy yet sweet, and the vegetables earthy and filling. I finished off everything on my plate then sat back. I'd gotten lost in the food and it had provided me a moment of reprieve from my frustration over not having figured out much more about the case.

Bridget Willows was a pseudo-business and life coach and had been the last person to see Tina alive, apart from Officer Miller. I'd have to add him to my suspect list at this rate. Josie didn't want to talk and was up to something, whether that was murder or not, I didn't know. Mary Moosmin was taken by the wind like Rhiannon by Fleetwood Mac, and Mandy... I could talk to Mandy again.

But I felt like a dog chasing its tail.

A *meow* from the kitchen doorway drew my attention.

Sunlight waited for me. He flicked his tail —unusual, he was normally in a great mood— and meowed a second time.

"Just a moment, Sunlight," I said, and got up. "I need to clean my plate. Can't leave more mess for Lauren."

Sunlight proceeded to break into a volley of meows. I frowned, taking my plate and cutlery over to the kitchen sink. I made short work of cleaning up and stacking everything neatly then turned back to my suddenly vocal cat.

A white cat, speckled brown, had appeared next to Sunlight.

Wait a second.

That wasn't a white cat speckled brown. It was a chocolate brown cat covered in white dust. The cat *meowed* at me, and a shock bolted through my chest.

"Cocoa Puff? Is that you?" I walked over to the kitties and bent down. I ran my fingers through Cocoa's fur, bringing them up covered in flour. "How?"

Sunlight meowed again.

This was beyond suspicious.

I could buy that Sunlight might break the rules and head into the kitchen when nobody was around, try his luck and romp around in the flour. But Cocoa? He was set in his ways. He wouldn't break the rules, not even if Lauren cooed at him and offered him chicken from the kitchen sink.

Regardless, I got up and walked back into the kitchen. I tried the pantry door. Firmly locked.

Meow! Meow! Meow!

The consistent meows from Sunlight brought me back to the archway. "What is it, boy?" I asked. "What are you trying to tell me?"

Sunlight darted off down the hallway, past the base of the stairs and into the foyer. He pawed the library door open and entered, the tip of his ginger tail slipping out of sight.

"Sunlight?"

He poked his cute kitty face out again.

"OK. I'm coming." I followed my cat into the library.

Sunlight was already over at one of the bookcases. This particular bookcase drifted on an unseen hinge—it was the entrance to one of the inn's many secret passages and led to the attic. Gamma and I knew about this one and had already mapped it.

Sunlight darted through the gap between

the secret door and the wall and proceeded up the circular staircase and out of sight.

"Wait for me," I called.

I took the stairs one at a time, carefully, since the staircase was rickety, and stopped at the top.

The attic had a few windows that allowed in light, and the space was usually filled with an eclectic collection of antique furniture, both covered by sheets and exposed. But recently, Gamma had left the doorway ajar so she could get help moving everything out to clear the area.

A man had "died" up here—a long story—and fascination about what had happened had made this an important part of her new ghost tour.

Except the attic wasn't empty.

It was filled with bags of flour. A few of them had torn and spilled their floury insides to the wooden boards.

Sunlight sat down beside me and meowed. An "I told you so" meow that I deserved.

"Good job, Sunlight," I whispered,

bending and stroking his furry ears. "Good job."

But what on earth?

Where had this flour come from? Lauren would lose it when she saw it sitting up here, unused and ill-looked after. The open bags were contaminated, and the rest? Was this where the supply had gone in Gossip? We hadn't had more of Lauren's waffle cupcakes for days.

"We've got to tell them about this," I said, and pulled my phone out of my pocket. I dialed my grandmother's number.

"Charlotte? We're about to pull up in front of the inn. What's the matter?"

"I've found Gossip's missing flour supply," I replied. "Technically, Sunlight's the one who found it."

"You what? Where?"

"In the attic. There's bags and bags of flour in the attic. The secret attic attached to the library."

"We're on our way up. Give us five minutes."

I had a fruitless staring competition with

the bags of flour. How had they gotten up here without anyone knowing? And when? And why?

Footsteps on the stairs came a couple of minutes later. Gamma and Lauren entered the attic and their jaws dropped.

"What on earth?" Gamma shook her head.

Lauren was speechless, though the flush in her cheeks said she was angry. "This is where the flour went? What the—? I'm going to strangle Billy for this. I thought he didn't have any from his suppliers but he must've sold it to someone." Lauren stormed toward the stairs. "I'll give that toad a piece of my mind!"

"Careful on the stairs," I called.

Lauren didn't reply but descended slowly, grumbling under her breath.

"What do you make of it?" I asked.

"I'm not sure what to make of it, Charlotte. This attic has been open all week, and the last time I came up here was five days ago to check it was neat. Somewhere between then and now, somebody has smuggled in countless bags of flour, right under my nose."

She was stiff. "I take the greatest offense to this. How didn't I see it?"

"You can't be everywhere at once," I said. "You've been busy with the kitten foster center."

"It's not an excuse. Things are going to change around here. I have a camera installed in the armory. It's about time I install a few around the outside of the inn."

I hadn't seen my grandmother this upset since Jessie Belle-Blue had waggled a newspaper in her face months ago and called the Gossip Inn a murder hotel. Something had to give.

❧ 20 ❧

"You're crazy, Billy. You're out of your mind. How could you sell my flour to somebody else?" Lauren was on the warpath. I didn't blame her if her supplier had sold her pre-ordered stuff to another buyer.

The chef paced back and forth in the inn's kitchen, one hand on her pregnant stomach, the other clasping her cell phone to her ear.

Gamma and I entered and took seats at the kitchen table. It wouldn't be long until the dinner service, and in the meantime, we didn't have much to do but consider the mystery of the reappearing flour.

And Tina's death.

I pulled my phone out and set it on the tabletop while Lauren raged .

"Case notes?" Gamma asked.

I opened them for her, and she scooted closer, reading over my shoulder as I made adjustments.

Victim Name: *Tina Rogers.*

Victim Detail: *Baker. In legal trouble. Hired me to prove her innocence—accused of breaking into The Little Cake Shop owned by Josie Carlson.*

Cause of Death: *Murder. Weapon unknown. Potentially poisoning. Confirmation required.*

Suspects

Josie Carlson

Mandy Gilmore

Bridget Willows

Officer Miller?

Evidence

Glove embroidered specially for Tina found in Josie's bakery—**embroidered by Mary Moosmin who is on vacation.**

Brownie at crime scene. **Still nothing on this.**

Links

Josie owned a bakery. Brownie was found next to the victim's hand. **Someone attacked Josie in the alleyway.**

Tina's glove was found in Josie's bakery. Tina claimed the glove wasn't hers. **Need to talk to Mary Moosmin about this when she's back from vacation.**

Someone who visited Tina must've killed her. **???**

Connection of Tina's "crime" to the murder? **Still nothing.**

Questions

<u>Who baked the brownies?</u>

<u>Did the brownies contain poison?</u>

<u>What was the cause of death?</u>

<u>What did Officer Miller hear?</u> **Nothing of note. Unless he's lying.**

<u>Who was the owner of the glove found in Josie's bakery if not Tina?</u>

<u>What was Mandy talking about to Detective Goode? What funeral?</u>

<u>Why did Mandy visit Tina?</u>

Why did Josie lie about visiting Tina?

And why did Bridget Willows, head of the Gossip Sewing Club, visit Tina? **Visited to discuss business mentoring and her arrest. Saw nothing.**

Was Brick Jonas involved in Tina's demise?

Who attacked Josie and why?

"You have a lot of unanswered questions, Charlotte."

"I know. Apparently, I'm not that good at this sleuthing thing," I replied.

"You're not serious," Lauren said, cutting across our conversation. "Fine. OK. Yeah, Billy. Yeah. No, I won't." She hung up on her supplier with a stab of her thumb and stared us down. "He didn't sell anyone my flour. Apparently, his supplier is fresh out too."

Gamma and I didn't say anything.

"What's the problem?" Lauren asked, directing that question at me, snappily.

My face went hot. "I, uh, we can't figure out why Mandy Gilmore visited Tina on the morning of the murder."

"That? Why didn't you just ask her? I did."

"You did?"

"Well, sure," Lauren said, relaxing out of her funk an iota. "After you mentioned it, I thought I might help you out by talking to her. She was in the same year as Josie so... yeah. I asked."

"What did she say, Lauren?" Gamma asked.

"That she visited Tina because she wanted to discuss Mr. Tindell's funeral. Apparently, they planned on attending it together. They were close, Tina and Mandy, and Mr. Tindell was a friend of the family, apparently. Mandy's and Tina's."

"Oh." I typed that out.

Perhaps, it was a good thing Lauren had asked instead of me. I doubted I would've gotten a candid answer from Mandy. But knowing her supposed reason why didn't make it true. Same as with Bridget Willows. She could easily have lied to me about her motivations.

Gamma and Lauren engaged in conversation about the appearance of flour in the attic, and I took to an online search about my suspects. Mandy's name brought up nothing but a few social media profiles, as did Josie's, but Bridget...

Jackpot. I knew there was something strange about her whole businesswoman act.

Bridget Willows had a previous criminal conviction. The Gossip Police Station had posted her mugshot online, dating back fifteen years ago. The charge? Aggravated assault.

"—a ghost put the flour in the attic." I tuned back into the conversation.

"Lauren, you have ghosts on the brain," Gamma said.

"Can that happen?" Lauren massaged her temples.

My grandmother *tut-tutted*.

"I'm sorry, I'm just worried about tonight."

"What's happening tonight?" I asked.

"Jason's going out of town, and I'm going to be alone at home with Tyson. I'm afraid of what might happen. What if the ghost comes upstairs and attacks? They can float through solid objects, you know. My grandmother always told me to watch out for that kind of thing."

"Is this the same grandmother who died and came back as a ghost?" Gamma asked, pointedly.

"I'm serious," Lauren said. "It's spooky what's going on at my house. If y'all don't believe me, then I don't know... come see for yourself."

"That's an excellent idea. Charlotte," Gamma said, "why don't you go over and stay at Lauren's tonight?"

"What's huh?"

"Go stay at her place tonight. You girls can chat and have a movie night. Keep her company. What do you say?" Gamma asked.

"Sure. Yeah, sure." It would get me out of the inn and stop me from obsessing over the evidence I didn't have. Or I could use the time to press Lauren for information about her sister. "Sure that would be fun."

"Great!" Lauren clapped her hands. "We can have a ghost hunt. I'll look up ways we can get rid of spirits. Or maybe we can communicate with it."

Oh boy. This ought to be fun. It would be an interesting night, at least.

❦ 21 ❦

Later that night...

"I'm afraid I didn't know, Charlie," Lauren said, stirring the pot of macaroni and cheese on the stovetop in her kitchen. Her house was cozy, the living room small but populated with neat furniture and a coffee table that held mostly baby toys. "It was before my time."

I'd asked Gamma about Bridget Willows' shady past, and she'd promised to do her own research and revert back to me with information. She'd had the assault record on file, but not any detail about it. I'd be interested to find out the truth.

"It's difficult to believe that Mrs. Willows would hurt anybody though," Lauren continued, tapping the side of her spoon on the pot. Apparently, macaroni and cheese was the perfect ghost hunting cuisine. I'd been informed of that the minute we'd gotten through the door.

Tyson was asleep in his stroller in front of the muted TV, his chubby arm thrown above his head.

"But that's always the case." I sat down on the sofa, watching Lauren's little boy as he snoozed. Amazing how kids were so cute when they weren't pooping or puking or crying.

"What do you mean?"

"Everybody thinks they *know* everyone else until the truth comes out."

Lauren lifted her hand and whispered behind it. "You *would* say that because you were an s-p-y." She spelled the letters out.

"I'm pretty sure if anyone's listening they can crack that code."

She blushed but took my jab in the spirit it was meant. Playful. "Oh, Charlie, I hope you can work out what happened to Tina soon. Everyone in Gossip's been so tense about it."

"I know," I said. "And I'll figure it out." I had to be confident about it, even though the case had presented me with some issues.

So far, my main suspect wouldn't talk, following her had yielded nothing, and no one would give me dirt on her. For all intents and purposes, everybody who had known Tina had been friends with her, apart from Brick, who was about as approachable as, well...

"I believe in you, Charlie. After everything you've been through, there's no way you won't get there in the end."

I appreciated the vote of confidence. The longer it took me to figure this out the more my sense of inadequacy grew. I'd gone from spy to maid, and while there was nothing wrong with being a maid, what good was any of my training now?

I had chosen to stay in Gossip because I'd

felt at home, but there was nothing but aching boredom and the feeling that I didn't have a real place here.

And the thought of anything happening to the people of this town set my stomach churning. I'd already landed my friends and the people I cared about in hot water once before. It had taken me a long time to warm to this town, and now that I had, there was no way I'd let anyone jeopardize that.

Especially not handsome detectives who think they know best.

Goodness, where had that thought come from?

"So," I said, to distract myself from morose thoughts, "what time does this mystery ghost usually start rocketing around down there." I gestured off to the basement door.

"Oh, it'll be soon." Josie checked her watch. "It happens every other night at 10:00 p.m.."

"Every other night?"

"Sure. Tuesdays, Thursdays, and Saturdays."

"A punctual and reliable ghost."

"Now, don't tease me, Charlie. It's real, I tell you," Lauren said, and brought the pot of macaroni cheese over to the counter. She doled spoonfuls into two waiting bowls.

"I wouldn't dream of—"

Something *crashed* in the basement. A clattering noise followed.

"See!" Lauren hissed. "I told you!"

Well, color me cream and call me Alfredo sauce.

A clatter sounded below and then silence ensued.

"I told you. I told you," Lauren repeated, and lifted her cheesy wooden spoon. She gripped it in both hands. "What do we do? What if it comes up here?"

"Wait here," I said.

"Charlie, you can't go down there by yourself."

I shushed her and headed for the basement door. What we had here was a wild animal. It had to be. As much as I'd like to get onboard the ghost train—not literally, that would be terrifying—I couldn't believe this was a paranormal occurrence.

My phone was in my hand, so I switched

on the flashlight app, covering the light with my thumb, then unlocked the basement door, quietly.

I sneaked down the steps, sticking to the edges to avoid most of the creaks and complaints, holding my phone at the ready.

A murmuring noise drew my attention, followed by a soft shuffling of feet. Close by.

I reached the basement floor. Dark shapes moved underneath the house, and my heart climbed into my throat.

"Freeze," I yelled, flashing the light on...

Two people in a passionate embrace!

They sprang apart, immediately.

Josie, plump, dark-haired, and coloring bright red.

And Brick? Brick Jonas, the massive football-wielder who had dodged my questions and had proposed to Tina before her death.

Lauren rattled down the stairs behind me then sucked in a breath. "Josie? What are you doing here?"

Brick grumbled and scuffed his shoe on the ground. "I, uh, I gotta get going." And then he clambered out of the basement window, an obscene spectacle to observe given the size of the man and the window respectively.

"Josie," I said. "This is why you went to visit Tina, isn't it?" The realization struck home hard. "You didn't want anyone to know that you were dating Brick, did you?"

She bowed her head, refusing to meet my eye.

"You were dating him while Tina was still his girlfriend, weren't you?"

Josie didn't reply.

"And you went to see her, why? To rub it in her face? Is that why you accused her of breaking into your bakery? You wanted her out of the way?"

"No! No, that was the truth. She did break in. I was sure she did, but I... look, I went to talk to her at the police station to tell her there were no hard feelings. And ask if she felt the same way. It wasn't a malicious meeting."

"Then why didn't you say so?" I asked.

"I didn't want people knowing about Brick. He's... well, he's dumb as mud. I like him, but it's embarrassing. And also, people liked Tina a lot. What would they say if they knew I stole him from her?"

"Josie Marie Carlson," Lauren said, "you should be ashamed of yourself! Running around in the middle of the night with a man. And hiding out in my basement to canoodle? It's disgusting. You get your butt upstairs, right this instant."

Josie didn't so much as look her sister's way. She trudged up the stairs, her head still down and her cheeks flaming red.

Lauren followed her up, scolding. "Never in all my years have I encountered someone who..."

I tuned it out.

Josie had been at the prison to talk to Tina about Brick. That left Mandy and Bridget.

Two suspects and two missions. It was time I gave my grandmother a call.

❧ 22 ❧

"Accoording to my Intel," Gamma said, from the driver's seat in her SUV, "Mrs. Willows attacked another businesswoman at a conference twenty years ago."

"Oh?"

"There was a dispute about money," my grandmother continued, reading off her phone, eyes narrowed, "but there aren't too many details about the cause. What my sources do remember is that she walloped the other woman repeatedly with an umbrella. Bruised her black and blue and sent her to hospital with a concussion."

"So, she has a temper," I said. "Not the type who would poison a person then."

"Still no cause of death?"

"Nothing. Nothing in the news. No press conference revealing what happened. Detective Goode and the sheriff are keeping this close to their chests." I wriggled my nose. "I detest a control freak."

"Stunningly ironic."

"I'm not a control freak."

"Then why are you so obsessed with the case?"

"I'm being paid to be obsessed with the case, Georgina. You know that."

She waggled a black gloved finger at me. "Don't be sassy, Charlotte. I'm here to help."

My grandmother had a commanding presence, and I didn't dare backchat. I'd wind up feeling and looking like a child. Not that there was anyone to witness as we had parked in the blacked out SUV under a tree across from Bridget Willows' tiny house.

"I'm not a control freak," I muttered, somewhat petulantly. At least I was aware of my petulance.

"I understand you, Charlotte. I understand what you're going through." My grandmother glanced out of the window at Mrs. Willows' darkened front yard. The porch lights were off. "You're not the only one who left a life of espionage and excitement behind. Gossip is slow. And your life was fast."

I didn't say a word. Gamma had torn my BandAid off in one sharp tug.

"It's not easy." Her sigh was fraught with memories. "Feeling as if you're useless after being respected and *needed* for years. Sort of like a professional Empty Nest Syndrome. But you'll get through it. Just don't kill yourself trying to solve mysteries and help other people to make yourself feel better about... Gossip."

I bit down on the inside of my cheek. It was an ego knock to admit any of what she'd said out loud. "Thanks," I managed.

"She's not home. You should go in."

"Alone?"

"You want the excitement, don't you?" My grandmother flashed me a grin. "No alarm beams, and a small house. Child's play." She popped the center console open with a tap of her fist. Gamma removed a silver bullet and placed it on my gloved palm. "Skeleton key. Hit the button on the side, slip it into the keyhole, and it will do the rest."

I turned the object over in my hand. "Got it."

"And here." Gamma removed a tube of lipstick next. She opened it, revealing the wedge of red lipstick within. "A woman's best friend. Looks like lipstick, but..." She closed the tube again, tapped once on the top and lifted it to show the bottom. A lens had been revealed. "Tap once on the lid to reveal the lens, one twist to take a photo. There's micro-SD card within." She handed that over too.

"Cool."

"Try not to get caught, Charlotte." She tapped her throat, and her voice sounded in my earpiece. "I'll warn you if she returns."

I slipped out of the SUV and headed across the road, keeping to the shadows. I'd opted for all-black tonight, but not armor. If I was caught, I didn't want the advanced technology exposed. Even if it was to a small town business woman with a rap sheet.

I reached the front of the house, tapped the silver bullet and exposed a section of metal. I inserted it into the door. The bullet made a nearly imperceptible hum and the clack of the lock followed.

Nice.

I pushed my way in and shut the door behind me. The last thing I needed was Bridget to arrive home and suspect something was up because I'd left the front door ajar.

The inside of the house was cramped. Living room, kitchen, hallway, bathroom, one bedroom. I made for the bedroom, keeping the lights off and avoiding the blocky shapes of the bed and dresser. I reached the window, opened it then closed the curtains.

Easy escape route. And I could now switch on the bedroom lights without anyone seeing who was in the room.

I hit the lights, squinting and allowing my eyes to adjust to the change.

Laptop on the bedside table.

It was facing the bed, so I positioned myself, touching nothing except the floor with my feet. I lifted the lid of the laptop carefully, and the screen lit up. No password. Bingo.

I navigated to the mailbox and opened it.

It was full of emails from members of the sewing club and various business contacts. I typed Tina's name into the search bar and several email threads popped up.

Re: Conference Booking for July

Hi Mrs. Willows,

Thanks for letting me know about this. I wanted to attend but I don't think I can afford it right now. The bakery has been struggling a little lately, and I want to keep up with my mentorship fees to you. I hope that's OK.

Tina.

...

On Wed, Jun 30, 2021 at 9:22 PM Bridget Willows (bridgewillowsbiz@bizmail.com)

Hi Tina,

I'm forwarding you an invitation to the Businessperson's Conference 2021 for Bakers. Please find all the relevant information attached. You can make the payment of $2999 to my bank account, and I *will forward that on to them and ensure your spot is secured.*

Have a good day, dear.
Mrs. Bridget Willows
Business leader to business leaders.

"Uh oh," I murmured.

That sounded scammy as heck.

Asking Tina to pay her for the "Businessperson's Conference 2021 for Bakers"? Yeah, that didn't even sound like a real conference. Had Bridget gone to see Tina to push her for money? Could it be that she'd gotten mad about it?

I lifted the lipstick tube and snapped a few photos of the correspondence. It would take less time to take photos than it would to forward this to myself.

"Come in, Chaplin," my grandmother spoke in my earpiece, quietly.

"Reading you, Big G."

"Suspect is inbound. Repeat. Suspect inbound. Get out of there, Chaplin, now."

"Copy." I exited the email app, closed the laptop and hit the lights.

A key scraped in the front door, the

sounds of Bridget murmuring under her breath as she tried to get into the house were the backdrop to my escape.

I opened the curtains, soundlessly, slipped out of the open window, turned and closed it. The light flickered on in the bedroom two seconds after I'd clicked the window into place. I bent low, keeping out of sight, and watched as Bridget entered the room. She dumped her purse on the bed then stretched, sat down and removed her shoes.

That was my cue.

23

I rounded the house, keeping low to the side of the building, my eyes peeled for activity from the neighboring yards or windows. "All clear?" I asked.

"For now. You'd better move quickly, Chaplin. There's someone rounding the bend."

I vaulted the fence, stripping off my gloves as I headed toward my grandmother's SUV. The person "rounding the bend" as she'd put it, walked authoritatively. They were tall and male, and they stopped after a few steps, spotting me standing next to the black SUV.

"Miss Smith?" Detective Goode's voice made my heart leap and then sink like a stone.

"I did tell you to hurry," my grandmother chirped in my ear. "Now, I'm going to have to leave you here. Tell him you have no idea who drives the car." The SUV's tires squealed on asphalt as my grandmother put the car in reverse, did a professional handbrake turn, and sped off down the road.

I would've been grumpy about the abandonment but my grandmother was right.

If I hadn't stopped to watch Mrs. Willows enter the room, hoping I'd see something incriminating, I'd have arrived at the SUV fast enough to evade Goode's detection.

"Miss Smith?" he repeated.

"Hi," I said, mentally searching for a reason to be here. "Did you see that car?" I tucked my gloves into the back pocket of my black pants, where I'd already secreted the skeleton key and lipstick camera.

"I sure did," Detective Goode replied, stopping under the vignette of light from a lamppost a few feet away. "What are you doing out here so late?" His tone was pleasant enough, but there was a definite edge to it. Suspicion.

I walked over to him, stopping under the light as well. It would, hopefully, set him at ease. What sneak in their right mind would stand in full view under a lamppost?

"I was visiting a friend." I gestured vaguely down the road.

"In that getup?"

"My fashion choice isn't to your liking?" I asked. "I'm so deeply scarred."

"I didn't mean to offend," Goode said, raising an eyebrow. "All black is not a common choice around here at this time of night."

"So, you're an expert, I see."

"Open hostility." Goode's remark was off-hand, he turned his head and looked directly at Mrs. Willows' house. "That's not the usual reaction I get from women."

"Oh yeah? I'm glad I could break the mould for you, Detective."

"As long as that's the only thing you're breaking."

The rising tension between us was almost too much to bear. I wanted to punch him right on the nose, but that would be a seriously bad idea. "What are you doing here?" I asked him, pointedly. "You don't live on this street. Do you?" I added in the question belatedly because my grandmother had already told me where the detective lived. So I could avoid him.

And it wasn't on this street.

"Just taking an evening stroll," he said.

I couldn't call him out on it without exposing that I knew he lived on the other side of town. "OK. Well, I guess I'll be on my way. Unless you plan on pulling me in for questioning or arresting me for visiting a friend."

"Not tonight, Miss Smith." He lingered, staring at me, his green eyes cutting right through to my soul.

"How's the investigation going?" Why not poke him for information while I had him here?

Detective Goode's expression closed off.

"I heard that Tina was poisoned. Is that true?" I had heard no such thing, but I needed the cause of death already. The radio silence about the case had gotten under my skin.

"No, it's not."

I didn't let my shock at him openly admitting that stop me from a follow-up question. "What happened to her then?"

"You expect me to tell you that?"

"Yes. I saw her body. I'm a witness. Don't you think I deserve a little closure?"

The detective snorted a laugh. "No."

"You're delightful. Has anyone ever told you that?"

"Look, I'll let you in on a secret. I don't care about being delightful or keeping the peace. I get the feeling you don't either."

So much for pretending to be the cowed maid from the Gossip Inn. The man triggered my anger in a big way.

"But I'll tell you the cause of death. We're releasing that information to the press tomorrow anyway. No use hiding it anymore. Mrs. Rogers was shot through the bars of her holding cell."

I couldn't keep a straight face.

"You don't believe me?"

"I can't figure out how Officer Miller wouldn't have heard a gunshot," I said. "Or anyone else in the building. It's a police station. Even with a silencer, that's still a lot of noise, especially in a tiled room."

"You know a lot about firearms?"

"I know enough," I replied. "It's good to stay educated."

"About weapons."

"It's a free country."

"And you should thank your lucky stars you're a free woman."

"Is that a threat?" I asked.

"Of course not," he replied, scanning me. "I don't make threats." He brushed past me, dousing me in his lemony cologne, and I hated that he smelled good.

"So, how come nobody heard the shot?" I called after him. "You ever think of that?"

"Small gun and a suppressor. Makes more of a knocking noise."

"Yeah, I know how it works, but Miller? What about Miller?" I asked. "He would've heard. Detective!"

But Detective Goode merely raised a hand as he sauntered off.

Darn him.

24

The following morning...

I glugged back a cup of coffee in the kitchen, standing over the sink. My eyes were scratchy from lack of sleep, and I couldn't help yawning every other minute. Lauren had banished me to the sink because I'd nearly cut my finger off chopping fruit for the breakfast parfait.

Gamma was in the kitten foster center,

dealing with a cat related emergency. Apparently, two of the kitties didn't get along and had to be separated. Of course, Mr. Grote, the uppity cat owner was in an absolute state about that.

Meanwhile, the guests had gathered outside waiting for their breakfasts and coffee while I tried desperately to keep it together.

I hadn't gotten much sleep last night. What with the news that the brownies weren't relevant to the crime, how was I meant to? Tina had been shot in her cell and nobody had heard a thing. It was a miracle Officer Miller had kept his job.

But who had shot her?

Bridget Willows? It had to be, right? Because Bridget had been the last one to see her alive.

Then again, if Officer Miller hadn't heard the shooting, he couldn't have been at his post. Someone might've sneaked into the holding cell area, apparently the Gossip Police Station couldn't afford simple cameras, and shot her when no one was around.

And that meant it could've been *anyone*.

Not just Mandy, Josie or Bridget. But anyone with a gun.

It wasn't like I could track down every licensed weapon owner in the town.

My head throbbed, and I forced another swig of coffee down my gullet.

"Do most people have guns?" I asked, more to myself.

"In Gossip?" Lauren replied. "Sure. A lot of people have guns. There are a lot of folks who like going hunting. Mr. Tindell liked hunting before he died. And that Brick Jonas too. Mrs. Marshall from the General Store, and—"

"No, small guns. Handguns."

"I don't know, Charlie, sorry."

I sighed, and massaged the tight knots of muscle that had formed in my shoulders.

"Charlie, honey, you look tired. Maybe you should let Detective Goode handle this one."

"No," I snapped it out. "Sorry, Lauren. I'm on edge. But no, I'm not letting *that* detective handle anything."

"Why not? He seems like he knows what he's doing."

I chose not to reply. My tongue was barbed and tasted of coffee this morning. And I just didn't *get* it. Josie had been meeting with Brick, betraying her friend Tina and shutting her out. Bridget had been pushing Tina for money. Mandy was apparently Tina's bestest friend in the world. There had to be an answer that made sense.

My brain felt like a sodden sponge.

"Mind getting out there and pouring coffees, Charlie?" Lauren asked, gently.

"Yeah. Right, of course. Sorry." I grabbed a full coffee pot and pushed out of the swinging kitchen doors. The guests were seated at their tables, chatting pleasantly, except for one. Opal stood beside Mandy's table, her arms folded and her face a thunderhead.

Uh oh. What's that about?

I made my way over, trying not to be obvious about it, stopping to fill coffee mugs on the fly.

"—think you're something special now. You're going to fail, just like you did before," Opal growled.

Mandy offered her an arrogant grin in return. "Jealousy doesn't suit you well, Opal. You've aged about ten years in the last ten seconds."

"How dare you! You horrible little witch. You think that—"

"Everything all right here?" I asked, stopping next to their table.

Opal didn't reply.

"Everything's perfect, thank you. Though, I could use some coffee." Mandy was the cat that got the cream this morning. She wore a long black dress, modestly cut, and was practically purring as she shifted her mug toward the edge of the table. "Opal was telling me how excited she is about my new acquisition."

"I was doing no such thing."

"Acquisition?" I asked.

"Why yes. I'm taking over The Bread Factory. Mrs. Rogers sold it to me because she's struggling to keep up with the cost of running the place, and I was more than happy to help her. The poor woman didn't even charge me that much for it." Mandy sighed.

I blinked, trying to absorb that information into the brain sponge upstairs. Mandy had bought The Bread Factory. That was... good? Bad? Suspicious. I wasn't even sure anymore.

"Don't get too excited," Opal put in, touching two fingers to my forearm. "Mandy's last business failed. Isn't that right, Mandy? You failed in business. That's the reason you returned to Gossip."

"I returned to Gossip because of Mr. Tindell's passing," Mandy replied, sharply. "It had nothing to do with business."

"So why not come for the funeral and then leave afterward?"

"I don't need to explain myself to you," Mandy said, her gaze flickering my way. "But for reference, if you must know, Mr. Tindell was a family friend and his death reminded me of what I'm missing out on here. A life with my family and friends."

"Liar." Opal rolled up the sleeves of her cotton shirt. "You're a liar."

"OK, that's enough," I said, finally bringing myself to the present. "Come on, break it up. People are trying to enjoy their breakfasts."

"How dare you talk to me like that!" Opal spun toward me.

She was right. I'd forgotten my "sweet maid" filter thanks to exhaustion. Also "how dare you" was Opal's favorite phrase.

"You," Opal said, pointing a finger in the vicinity of my chest, "will not talk to *me* like that. You're just a lowly maid. I'll report you to your boss."

I considered my options. If I grabbed this woman's finger and twisted it I'd get in a lot of trouble. But would the satisfaction of teaching her a very visceral lesson outweigh the costs? Probably.

"There's no need to get angry," I said.

Opal puffed up, extending her height so she towered over me.

Note to self. Don't tell an angry woman not to get angry.

"You little—"

A throat cleared, and Opal froze. She looked past me, and the fury drained from her face. She shrank back to her normal size, putting up a helpless smile and rearranging her ginger curls. "Oh, hello, Detective. I didn't see you there."

Detective? Not this guy again. I turned toward the dining room's archway, and there he was. Detective Goode with his lanyard around his neck.

He nodded to me. "Have a minute, Miss Smith?"

This is going to be bad.

❧ 25 ❧

Detective Goode led the way, another point that annoyed me, and stopped in front of the library door. "Can we talk in here?" he asked, gesturing to it.

"Sure. Why not? We can talk anywhere *you* want."

"Good."

I gritted my teeth. I'd walked right into that one. Either Goode was incredibly annoying or I was tired or it was a combination of both.

We entered my favorite spot in the inn and the detective took a seat in an armchair, gesturing for me to do the same. Cocoa Puff had planted himself on the arm of one of the chairs, so I chose that one, and stroked him, his fur soft and warm. I'd brought the coffee pot in with me, so I shoved it onto the coffee table.

Deep breaths. Don't attack an officer of the law. Sheesh, what is with me today? Why does this guy bother me so much?

"What do you want to talk about?" I asked.

"We've gone over what you saw at the police station on the day of Tina's death," Detective Goode said, "but there are some discrepancies between your account and Officer Miller's. I wanted to clarify a few things."

"OK. What discrepancies?"

"Timing. Whether you signed in or not. Things that were said. That kind of thing."

I glared at him. "You can't seriously think I had anything to do with this. I arrived after Tina had been killed. Surely, your medical examiner would know that?"

Detective Goode had a great poker face.

"Are you going to cooperate with my questions, Miss Smith?"

"Of course."

"Then let's begin. I'd like you to walk me through exactly what happened. From start to finish. The more detail you give, the better."

"Is this an interrogation?" I asked. "You haven't read me my rights. If I'm under arrest, I want a lawyer."

"Why would you assume that?" Goode's smile was wry. "Miss Smith, I'm talking to you because you're a witness. There's no other reason. I need to get my timeline straight."

"Then you think Officer Miller is lying?"

"Let's start from the top." Detective Goode's continuing grin sent my blood pressure through the roof.

But I had no choice. I had to cooperate. If I didn't, it would make things worse for me.

❧

THANKFULLY, DETECTIVE GOODE HADN'T kept me for too long. He'd made me recount my statement, asked me a few questions, then thanked me for my time, all with that frustrating grin on his handsome face.

No. Not handsome. Annoying.

Lauren and I finished up the breakfast service without much trouble. Mandy and Opal had retreated to their corners, and the food had gone down as well as it always did. Eggs, bacon, sausages, biscuits and gravy, grits, but with nothing sweet afterward because of the flour shortage. The chef had refused to even consider using the flour we'd found upstairs. I didn't blame her.

I removed the last of the plates from an empty table then entered the kitchen through the swinging doors.

"I don't care, Billy." Lauren clutched her phone to her ear. "I want the number. Give me the number. Billy, I swear, if you don't give me the number I'm going to come down there and make your life miserable. Do not mess with a pregnant woman."

I washed off the plates while the argument continued and stacked them in the dishwasher. Everyone was in a foul mood today. A dark cloud hanging over the inn?

"Good. Yeah, I've got a pen." Lauren snatched one up from next to her recipe book and wrote down something at the top of the page. It had to be serious if she was willing to desecrate her recipe book like this. "Got it. Yeah, yeah. Bye!" She hung up and practically tossed her phone aside. "Finally!"

"What's that?" I asked.

"That is the address of the Gossip Stone-ground Flour Mill," Lauren said. "They're the ones who supply Billy, and since Billy's the one who supplies me, he didn't want to give out their details. Apparently, the number is top secret but he caved on giving me the address. Now, I get to go down there and give them a piece of my mind about not supplying him with any flour." Lauren clutched her head and let out a breath.

"Lauren? Are you OK?"

"Fine," she said, running a shaking hand through her bright red hair. "I'm fine. I'm just not good with all this stress. Josie's been acting strange lately, and the whole affair thing with Brick got under my skin, and the flour... One of the many joys I have is making cupcakes for everybody, and I can't even do that."

"Here. Sit down." I guided her to a chair then fetched her a glass of ice cold water. "You work too hard, Laur. You need to take some time for yourself. Relax."

"What I need to do is go down there and ask them what they think they're doing," Lauren said. "Selling out all the flour to someone else. Crazy." She sipped her water.

"No. Let me do it. Trust me, I could use the escape from the inn." And the escape from my thoughts. It was true that the best ideas came in the shower or moments before one fell asleep. When you were completely distracted.

And since I'd been on the brink of falling into a dead coma all morning, I was liable to come up with the next great invention. Or make a deduction about the case that would help us work out who'd killed Tina.

Gun. Bars. Officer Miller wasn't at his post. Not Bridget? Maybe Bridget. If not, then who? How did they get back in? Why? Mandy's bought the bakery. Mrs. Rogers?

The disconnected thoughts drifted through my mind, and I shook my head to clear it.

"Seriously. let me handle this."

"Are you sure you want to do that?" Lauren asked. "You've got so much on your plate already, and I don't want to be a nuisance."

"Don't be silly," I said. "You're the one who has a lot on her plate. I'll take care of the supplier, find out what's going on, and press them for an answer on when you'll get another shipment of flour."

"You're a hero, Charlie."

I wanted to swell with pride, but I didn't have it in me. So far, I wasn't a hero. I was a two-bit sleuth without a clue. And there was still a murderer on the loose.

"I'll be back soon," I said, stripping off my apron. "Tell Georgina I'll catch up with her when I'm back, OK? And that I took the Mini-Cooper again." And then I was off. Hopefully, to solve at least one of the mysteries the inn had cooked up for me.

❦ 26 ❦

The Gossip Stoneground Flour Mill was situated on the outskirts of town, along the river that ran past it. A brick building bearing the name of the mill in bold print across its side, it looked inviting for a place that made flour. And it was bigger than I'd expected.

I parked my grandmother's Mini-Cooper in an open spot in front of the doors and stifled a yawn. This would be a nice break from the investigation and the constant mental torture about who might've done what.

In essence, my suspect list had been reduced to zero, and I needed to figure out who had bought a gun and suppressor recently. But calling the gun shop in the neighboring town would likely raise suspicions since Detective Goode would've looked into that line of investigation already.

The last thing I needed was *another* visit from the detective.

I opened the cutesy wooden door of the mill, painted forest green, and found the reception area empty except for a young woman with a round face who sat behind a desk bearing the mill's signage. The reception area was carpeted, the brick walls exposed.

"Hello there," the receptionist said. "How may I help you today?"

"I'm here to lodge a complaint and talk to the owner of the mill. Or the manager. Whoever's here."

"Oh! Oh, OK. I'm sorry about the complaint. I-I, uh, give me a second. I'll get the manager for you." The receptionist pushed up from the desk and hurried through a back door.

I waited, circling the room and checking

out the pictures on the walls—images from the original establishment of the mill as well as pictures of the staff in action.

The door opened, and the receptionist returned, wringing her hands. She was followed by a lanky gentleman with a bushy mustache. He wore an apron and a plaid shirt.

"I hear you have a complaint, ma'am?"

"Nice to meet you," I said, extending a hand. "My name is Charlotte Smith. I'm from the Gossip Inn. You might've heard of it?"

"I have. Milton Bragg." He had a firm handshake, dry as the flour he milled. "What seems to be the problem?"

"Our chef usually gets flour from her supplier, Billy."

"Oh sure, I know Billy. He's a buyer of ours."

"Right," I continued, "except Billy doesn't have any flour. He's told us that you're refusing to sell to him."

"It's not so much that we're refusing to sell to him," Milton replied, "it's more that we don't have flour to sell at the moment. We're in the process of packaging more, so the flour supply should be back to normal next week." He removed a card from the pocket of his shirt and handed it over. "You can reach me here and buy directly from us if you want to get around your issues with Billy."

"Billy's not the issue per se. It's that there's no flour this week. What happened?"

Milton cleared his throat, Adam's apple bobbing up and down. "We, uh, well, that was the owner's decision."

"Meaning?"

"We had a woman come in and convince the owner of the mill to give her our current flour stock. She was offering to pay way above the usual rate. Way above. And he went for it. I didn't have a say, unfortunately, in the deal." Frustration laced his words.

"A woman," I said. "Do you know what her name was?"

"Jonas or something, right, Shelly?"

The receptionist nodded from behind the desk, sitting straight-backed and paying keen attention to our conversation.

"Jonas. Her last name was Jonas." *As in Brick Jonas? Brick's not married.*

"That was the name she gave. I think," Milton said. "Like I said, I wasn't involved in the deal. My part comes in filling the demand that we didn't meet."

"What did she look like, if I may ask?" A sneaking suspicion had descended upon me. Suddenly, my brain didn't feel as spongy and waterlogged.

"Dark hair?" Milton asked.

"She had dark hair," the receptionist put in, "and she was short, kind of plump. Really grumpy. Uh, yeah."

Josie. That's Josie. I know a grumpy, plump, dark haired Josie when I hear her. "Was she wearing an apron by chance?"

"Yeah. An apron with a smiling cartoon cake on the front."

"Thanks," I said. "I appreciate the information." And headed for the exit, a fire officially lit under my booty.

"Is that all?" Milton called. "Do you need anything else?"

"No, thank you. This conversation has been *exceedingly* helpful."

I darted toward my grandmother's Mini-

Cooper, my mind focused on the facts. Josie had bought all the flour, and Josie would have known where to store it. In the attic at the Gossip Inn. But why use Brick's last name? And why buy the flour in the first place?

I had a hunch. I just had to check that I was right.

❧ 27 ❧

I burst through the front door of The Little Cake Shop, drawing shocked cries from the customers in the line in front of me.

"Good heavens." Mrs. Stilt, a local librarian, clasped her pearls to her throat. "Is there any need for that? You nearly gave me a heart attack."

"We're not in the library any more, grandma." That had come from Archer, her grandson, who stood beside her, texting.

I ignored them and strode to the front of the line, zeroing in on the barista closest to me. She caught my eye and paled. I must've looked a sight, hair sticking up at odd ends, tired, and the whites of my eyes showing.

"Hi," I said, practically barking it out.

She spilled cream from a pitcher, murmured under her breath and started mopping it up with napkins. "I'm sorry," she said, "but *there's a line.*"

"A line?" Which line had I crossed this time? "Oh wait. Oh, you mean a queue? No, no, I'm not here for coffee. I want to know if Josie's around."

"Of course. She's in the office. But she's requested that nobody disturb her. I'm afraid no one's allowed back there."

I ignored the instruction and rounded the counter.

"Miss! Excuse me, Miss? You can't go back there. You can't—"

I burst through the office door, and Josie jumped at her desk, her hand flying to her throat. Her shock morphed into rage, immediately.

"Who do you think you are, barging into my office like this?" she growled, rising from her seat. "I can have you arrested. I'll call Officer Miller, right now and—"

"You'd like that, wouldn't you?" I swung the door shut in the face of the barista, who'd chased after me to no avail.

"What?" That got her attention. "What are you talking about, you crazy freak?"

"Officer Miller. He let you into the holding cell area after the last visitor, didn't he?" I posed the question in an icy tone. "He let you in, and then you shot Tina through the bars in cold blood."

Josie went white as fondant. "She was sh-shot?"

"Yeah, she was shot. And you know that she was shot because you did it," I said. "Isn't that right, Josie Jonas?"

Josie jerked back a single step at the use of the name. "I don't know what you're talking about. I didn't shoot Tina."

"But you were trying to put her out of business," I said, keeping the pressure up. "You bought all the supplies of flour from the mill that supplied her bakery." It was a wild guess, but the way Josie recoiled told me it was true. "And you used Brick's last name to hide your identity. Isn't that right?"

"Everything I've done has been for the good of the business," Josie said. "For The Little Cake Shop. You have no idea what it's like to run a bakery. To be in debt. To have external pressures from every direction, just closing in and—"

"That's what you spoke to her about when you visited her, wasn't it? It wasn't about Brick, it was about how you planned on bringing her down. And when she told you she wouldn't back off, you shot her."

"No!" Josie yelled.

"Miss Carlson?" the barista called through the door. "Are you OK in there?"

I turned the lock so she couldn't get in. If Josie was the murderer, she'd have the perfect opportunity to get rid of me too. Or she would have if I hadn't been a retired spy with training in hand-to-hand combat.

"I didn't kill Tina," Josie said. "I wouldn't throw away my life like that."

"The evidence points to you, Josie. And if you want to keep everything you have, I suggest you start talking." It wasn't a rational request, and I didn't have any accompanying power, but I had to trust my gut and go with it. Hopefully, Josie would be unnerved enough to respond.

"Look," Josie said, putting up her palms, almost backed into the corner, "this isn't what you think. I would never have hurt Tina. I was angry at her, but I would never have hurt her."

"Then what happened?"

"I... Tina wanted to buy me out, OK? She approached me with an offer. Apparently, this mentor person of hers had encouraged her to try and combine our businesses or something? It made me mad, so mad like... you wouldn't believe. And before you say anything, no I wasn't angry enough to murder her. But I was angry enough to say no. We had an argument about it."

"And then what happened?"

"Tina threatened to shut me down. She had no leg to stand on, but yeah. This was her idea of a grand joint venture. Buying me out. There's nothing joint about that!" Josie huffed.

"If she'd never met that idiot Bridget this wouldn't have happened."

"Where does the flour come into it?"

"I said I was angry, OK? I'm not great with my emotions. So, I tried to come up with a way to get back at her. I knew she was using stoneground flour for her bread, and that she thought it was the best possible type of flour around."

"So you went to the mill and bought it all?"

Josie nodded. "Just for the week. I wanted to teach her a lesson. I wanted her to realize that she couldn't just throw her weight around. The way she spoke to me made it seem like she was on top of the world with The Bread Factory, but now I hear she was on the brink of going out of business when... *it* happened. The murder." Josie took a breath. "And then the vandalism and the break-in happened. A lot of my equipment was stolen. And money. My bakery was trashed, and it cost a lot of money to fix it up. And, what with the glove and everything, I figured it had to be Tina who did it, right? So I reported her to the police."

"And she was arrested."

"Yeah. But I swear, I didn't hurt her. I swear. I would never risk my life and business like that. I-It would just be dumb."

"And the story you fed me about Brick?" I asked.

"That was true," Josie said, grimacing. "I like the guy. He's not smart or fancy or I dunno. He doesn't even have a great job, but I like him. And Tina didn't treat him right, and I did."

"What did you actually talk to Tina about on the morning of her murder?" I asked.

"Brick. Truthfully, I spoke to her about Brick. I was trying to clear the air, but she was not interested. Not at all. She told me to get lost. She threw a brownie at me."

"So it was you who brought her the brownies," I said.

"Yeah. I wanted to make peace."

"Why didn't you tell me?"

"Because I was afraid all of this would get out. And that Tina might have been poisoned or something," she said. "That would make *me* look like the one who'd done it. And I didn't. I really didn't."

"OK," I said, at last. "OK."

Josie sank into her office chair and planted her head in her hands. "This is such a mess. I can't believe she's gone. Even after what happened, I just—Tina was a friend. Even if we were frenemies, we were still close. It's weird not having her around. It's weird seeing The Bread Factory closed. And it's my fault, isn't it? I drove the final nail into the coffin." Josie sniffed, a single tear dropping onto her desktop.

"Josie, is there anything else you can tell me that would be relevant? Anything you were too afraid to tell me before?"

"Not really, no." Josie looked up. "That Officer Miller is a slacker, though. He didn't fetch me to end the visitation. He took a smoke break and let me walk out by myself. I didn't even see him after I'd signed in."

More evidence that anybody could've gotten past the man.

"Do you know anyone who has a gun?" I asked.

"What?"

"The killer shot Tina."

"I'm sorry, no."

"Are you sure that glove belonged to Tina? The one you found in your store?" I asked.

"I'm sure," she said. "Look. I've got the other one right here. I gave one to the police and kept one just in case." She opened her desk and produced a glove with a daisy on the front.

My eyes widened.

"What?"

"May I have that, please?"

"I guess. I don't have any use for it." Josie placed it on her desk.

I lifted the glove, my heart galloped in my chest. If Tina's mother had given me her glove, and the police had, supposedly, the other glove. Then whose glove was this?

❧ 28 ❧

Back at the inn, thirty minutes later...

I wrenched my bedroom door open and charged inside. Cocoa Puff followed me in and leaped onto my white comforter, settling in and purring away.

"I think I'm onto something," I said. "I'm onto something, Cocoa."

He meowed encouragement.

I opened the top drawer of my bedside table and wormed my fingers under the false bottom I'd installed recently. It popped free, and I removed the glove Tina's mother had given me from underneath and placed it on the bed.

Cocoa ignored my fevered movements, choosing to lick his unmentionables instead.

Beside Tina's glove with its white daisy embroidered on the front, I placed the glove Josie had given me. They were largely identical, but for one small detail. The center of the daisy on Tina's glove was orange, and the center on the mystery glove, found at the scene, was yellow.

These were two different sets of gloves. Belonging to different people.

Tina hadn't broken into Josie's bakery after all, and here was the proof.

I whipped my phone out and took a picture of both gloves then sent that to my grandmother with a follow-up text.

"Going to call Bridget Willows for contact details of Mary the glove maker. That's the key. Where are you?"

My grandmother's reply came through a minute later. "At the Gossip Cat Rescue Shelter. Will be back in a few hours. Take whatever you need from downstairs."

Downstairs was the armory. She knew I was on a roll.

I opened my contacts list and dialed Bridget Willows' number.

"This is Bridget Willows, businesswoman and mentor, how may I help you?" Bridget's voice was haughty, as if that would help draw people into her scheme. I'd become increasingly convinced that was what it was. Her business was a scheme, designed to draw in unsuspecting young people and get them to pay her vast sums of money. Though, I couldn't figure out what she was using that money for, given the state of her house.

"Mrs. Willows," I said. "It's Charlotte Smith." It was easier to say my fake name now, but I missed my true last name. Mission.

"Oh, hello, Charlotte, dear. How are you?"

"I'm calling about Tina's gloves," I said. "I wanted to know if you'd heard from Mary yet?"

"Actually, yes. Mary's with me right now.

She's been back from her vacation since late last night, isn't that right, Mary, dear?"

"May I talk to her please?"

"Now? We're in the middle of a conversation."

And I was in the middle of losing my patience. "Yes, please, now."

"I don't think that's appropriate, Charlotte."

"Give her the phone, please, Bridget."

"Charlotte, are you trying to tell *me* what to do?" Mrs. Willows was utterly shocked by the mere suggestion.

"Sorry, perhaps I wasn't clear enough," I said, my patience vanished, my goal in sight. "Hand Mary the phone or I will go down to the Gossip Police Station and tell them that you tried to extort over two thousand dollars from Tina for a bogus conference that didn't exist. Whether that's true or not won't matter because the police will look into the report. And they will, undoubtedly, find incriminating correspondence between you and Tina, and all the other women you've been taking advantage of. I'm sure there's an electronic trail. Or a paper one. Either way, the damage will be done once the news gets out in Gossip. You know how rumors spread in this town. Now hand over the phone."

A rustling followed my monologue and for a second I was sure that Bridget had hung up.

"Hello?" A soft voice like spun sugar. The woman on the other end sounded liable to melt in the rain.

"Is that Mary Moosmin?" I asked.

"Yes. Who is this?"

"I'm Charlotte Smith," I said. "And I had a question about the gloves you embroidered for Tina."

"Oh, yes, of course. Beautiful, aren't they?" Mary's smile was audible. "Poor Tina was so distraught when she lost one."

"Lost one?" I asked.

"Oh yeah, about a month ago, she misplaced one of her gloves. I was going to knit her another, but we didn't get around to it before my vacation."

So, that was why Tina's mother had only one of Tina's gloves. Ursula had likely believed that the other had been found at the crime scene. Not the case. "Tina's gloves," I said, "when did you make them?"

"Oh, years ago," Mary said. "Years. Just after she had graduated high school. Her and her best friend came to me because they wanted to get matching pairs of gloves. I convinced them they would need some differentiation between them or they'd be confused. Tina chose to have her daisy's floral disc colored orange, and her best friend chose yellow."

"Who was her best friend?" I asked.

"Mandy," she replied. "Mandy Gilmore, of course. The two were inseparable back then, but I believe they drifted apart. How sad. You know, Mandy always was a driven young woman, and I think she left Gossip to start her own bakery?"

"Bakery." The word dropped from my lips.

I had gone cold. To the tips of my fingers and toes.

"Bakery."

"Are you all right?" Mary asked. "Hello?" She tapped on the phone. "Hello?"

"Thank you," I managed, then hung up on her.

The clues in the case crashed together.

Mandy had bought the bakery from Ursula when she was at her lowest. Mandy had mentioned Mr. Tindell, and hadn't Lauren told me that Mr. Tindell liked hunting. And guns? Mandy and Tina had been friends, and Mandy had left town to start a bakery.

The gloves belonged to her.

"Cocoa," I croaked. "I've figured it out."

He purred in return.

"I have to catch her before it's too late." If Mandy would kill Tina in a police station to get what she wanted, there was no telling what else she might do.

❧ 29 ❧

The Rose Room was empty. Mandy Gilmore had already checked out. Either that was because she'd bought a home or moved in with a family member, but it didn't matter. She was gone.

Adrenaline raced through my veins, the certainty that she was the one who had killed Tina growing by the second. With her gone from the Gossip Inn, I had but one option. I would have to head to The Bread Factory and case the place out until she appeared.

I darted down the stairs in the Gossip Inn,

heading for the armory, and bringing my cell phone out of my pocket.

As much as I despised what I was about to do, Detective Goode deserved to know what I'd discovered. I prepared a text that I'd send off after I was fully prepared for the confrontation with Mandy. It was for my grandmother, asking that she give him the tip he'd need to arrest Mandy, anonymously.

My goal was clear.

Get to Mandy, question her, leave the recording of that questioning for the police, and ensure she was sufficiently detained. Thereafter, I'd return to Ursula with my results, and I'd give her back the money she'd paid me at the start of this.

She needed it more than I did.

I entered my grandmother's armory and picked out the relevant options for my mission.

Armor that went under my usual clothing —it was afternoon and a black get-up would make me stand out—as well as cable ties, a tranquilizer gun, a Taser, and pepper spray for good measure. All less lethal weapons than an actual firearm. But I strapped my Sig Sauer P365 to my side underneath my jacket.

It was time.

❦

I WALKED INTO TOWN, USING THE TIME TO calm my breathing, my senses heightening the closer I drew to The Bread Factory. It was a summer afternoon, and hot, but I couldn't take off my jacket without exposing that I had a gun strapped to my side. The rest of my "tools" were secreted in my purse. I wore gloves. Odd for this heat, but I didn't want my fingerprints muddying what I was about to do.

Folks smiled and greeted as they walked by, and I returned each of those greetings with similar enthusiasm.

This is it.

It was silly to be this nervous about a small-town murderer. Even if she had a hand-gun. I'd dealt with higher profile targets than this before, but this felt like the most important thing I'd ever done.

If I caught her, if I helped, it was like... the

pieces of the puzzle would fall into place. My life in Gossip would have meaning beyond my duties at the inn. I would no longer be, Charlotte Smith, maid or even Charlotte Mission, failed spy.

I approached The Bread Factory, my eyes peeled, and sat down on the bench opposite it, bringing my phone out of my purse and shooting off my prepared text to Gamma. I put my phone on silent right after then focused my attention on the bakery.

Down the road, Josie's cake shop was doing a roaring trade. The Bread Factory's doors were still closed, the red and brown awning drooping in the afternoon heat.

Movement inside drew my gaze.

She was in there.

Mandy walked back and forth in the store, talking on her phone and gesturing. She looked happy. She looked like a woman who thought she'd gotten away with murder.

I pushed up from the bench, checked the street both ways, then crossed at a leisurely pace. I knocked on the glass front door and smiled when Mandy caught sight of me.

"Are you open?" I called. "I could use a croissant."

"Just a sec." Mandy hung up the phone then unlocked the door and opened it a bit.

I pushed past her. "Oh thank goodness," I said. "I'm in desperate need of something to eat. Bread. Lauren at the inn can't make any. Flour shortage or something."

"Uh..." Mandy shut the door, the bell above it tinkling. "I'm sorry, uh, what was your name again? Charlotte?"

"That's right," I said, turning toward her with a smile, clutching my purse to my side.

"I'm sorry, but I'm not open. I've just bought the place so there's a lot to prepare."

"Oh. Oh, that's too bad. I was hoping to grab a bite."

"Sorry." Mandy shrugged then gestured to the door. "Thanks for stopping by, though. I'll be open next week, and you can come on down for a free croissant. How about that?"

"You're too kind." I walked toward her, smiling, and removed my phone from my pocket. "I guess I'll just look up another place where I can get bread. Seriously, I'm craving something doughy and delicious. Craft bread."

Mandy walked past me, offering nothing but an apologetic smile. I set my phone on one of the tables in The Bread Factory and hit the button to record. Then, I drew a second item out of my purse. The glove. Mandy's glove.

"Oh, by the way, I was talking to Josie earlier, and she gave me this to give to you." I held it out.

Mandy turned again, still with that vapid, nowhere smile on her face, and her gaze fell to the glove in my palm.

"It's yours, right?" I asked, tilting my head. "The glove?"

Her expression froze. "Where did you get that?"

"Josie gave it to me."

"Josie."

"You know, Josie from the bakery down the road? I think she found it in her store." Now was where it got real, and I kept my muscles relaxed, ready to act on instinct at a moment's notice. "I think you must have dropped it there when you were breaking in."

Mandy stared at me. "You. How?"

"You know, when you broke into her bakery and vandalized it because you wanted to open one of your own. Is any of this ringing a bell?"

Her fingers twitched at her sides.

"And when that didn't work, and Tina took the fall for the crime, you went to see her to stop her from outing you, correct?"

"How do you know any of this? Who *are* you?"

"You killed Tina, didn't you?"

Mandy backed away, shaking her head. She hit the counter and circled it, putting it between us, trembling. "I don't know what you're talking about."

"No?" I dropped the glove next to my phone, carefully. "You're sure about that? You sure you didn't borrow Mr. Tindell's handgun and suppressor?" That was a guess on my part. I had no idea where she'd gotten the gun from. "Didn't walk into the police station when Officer Miller was on one of his smoke breaks? Didn't take the gun and shoot Tina through the bars of her holding cell? Horrible way to go, don't you think? Her taking the fall for your crime and then being killed for it. Alone."

"She deserved it," Mandy hissed, finally snapping. She reached under the counter and produced the handgun in question, a Glock 19, the suppressor screwed onto the end. "She deserved everything that was coming to her. I tried to tell Tina not to get involved with Bridget, but she didn't listen and look where that got her."

"What's Bridget got to do with it?"

"Ah, so you don't know everything. Bridget took *my money* years ago. Gave me the same business conference turd talk that she did Tina, and I nearly lost everything. I decided to leave town, start up on my own."

"But you came back," I said. "Because you failed."

"Do you want to die too?" Mandy asked, aiming the gun at my chest. "That's where this is going, you know. You don't seem nearly afraid enough."

"Sorry about that," I replied. "So, what, you killed Tina because she knew you had broken into Josie's place? Why not kill Bridget? She's the one you were mad at."

"Tina wasted her money, and she wasted more of my money. I wanted to invest in her business. That's why I came back to Gossip. But when she told me what had happened, I saw red. I decided I'd open my own place. And I didn't need Josie for competition, or Tina for that matter."

"So you broke in and planted the glove. Stole what you needed. That right?"

"Correct," Mandy replied.

"And when Tina threatened to out you."

"I had enough," Mandy said, shaking the gun at me. "I had enough of everybody walking all over me. Bridget, Tina, that evil piece of work, Josie. All of them. So, yeah, I killed Tina Rogers. I'm proud of it. And now, I'm going to kill you. I'll say it was an accident. That I thought you were an intruder. That I shot you in self-defense."

"I don't think so," I said, and charged toward her.

Mandy's eyes widened, her finger squeezed the trigger. A muted *tap* came next, followed by a punch to my chest. Breath rushed from my lungs, and I stumbled back a step. I was trained for this. Mandy had shot me and the bulletproof armor under my clothes had saved my life.

That's going to bruise in the morning.

Mandy stared in horror as I ran her down. She let off two more shots, both going wide. I tackled her to the ground, swiftly, disarmed her with a twist of her wrist, then flipped her into a chokehold.

She gasped and tapped on my arms, clearly unnerved by how I'd handled the situation.

"Who-are-you?" she managed, before she lost consciousness.

I released her immediately, checked her pulse was normal, her chest rising and falling. I fetched my cable ties from my purse and fastened her arms and legs, before rolling her onto her side and ensuring her air passage wasn't restricted.

Mandy's phone was on the counter. I grabbed it, retreating to the table where I had set up the recording. Quickly, I edited and clipped the recording and played it back.

"I had enough of everybody walking all over me. Bridget, Tina, that evil piece of work, Josie. All of them. So, yeah, I killed Tina Rogers. I'm proud of it." Mandy's voice. Loud and clear.

I transferred that clip to her phone, then put it on the countertop and set it to play on a loop. I placed the glove next to it, then collected my things.

A car screeched to a halt outside. A black SUV.

I left Mandy on the floor and dipped out into the sunlight, checking no one had noticed my departure. Finally, I slipped into the interior of the SUV, greeting my grandmother with a grin.

"Detective Goode is on his way," Gamma said, tapping the radio attached to her dashboard. "They're going to arrest her."

"Good. I trussed her up like a turkey in there."

"There's sufficient evidence for her arrest?" Gamma asked, speeding off down the road, the windows tinted so dark that no one could see in.

"I'll say."

Sirens wailed, and a glimpse of the rearview mirror before we turned the corner showed me the cops pulling up in force in front of The Bread Factory.

After what had felt like a year, I could finally relax. I settled back into the SUV's comfy leather seat and closed my eyes.

Case closed.

❧ 30 ❧

One week later...

"The world is right again," Lauren sang, merrily, as she stirred the cupcake batter. "Y'all better be prepared for the best waffle cupcakes ever."

"I've been waiting all week," my grandmother said, primly, sitting at the kitchen table, the local newspaper, *The Gossip Rag,* open in front of her. "Whatever you make will only improve my mood."

The headline of the newspaper had annoyed my grandmother.

Local detective solves murder case! Detective Goode lauded as a hero.

There was no mention of my name in the article, and that meant I'd done my job correctly. Everything had gone to plan, from Goode finding Mandy to me returning the money to Tina's mother. And no one was the wiser about my involvement. The sign of a good spy.

But Gamma, for once, didn't see it that way. "Charlotte did nearly all the work, and this detective gets to sweep in and take all the credit?"

"I don't think it's his fault," Lauren said, setting her mixing bowl down on the countertop. "You know what that Jacinta at the paper is like. She takes a thread and runs with it."

"She can run into the end of a sharp pole," Gamma grumbled.

I patted her on the arm. "I don't care, Georgina. I'm just happy it's all over, you know? It's better that nobody knows about my involvement. Easier this way."

"If you say so, Charlotte. Sometimes, it doesn't hurt to stand out. Besides, everybody who's anybody in Gossip knows that you're the woman to talk to about fixing problems. Where's the use in hiding that?"

"They can know about it," I said, "as long as they don't have proof."

I sipped my coffee and let the atmosphere wash over me. The kitchen was cool this morning, though it promised to be a scorcher of a day, and Lauren chatted with us, telling us about the kicks from her baby last night, and how Tyson and Jason had gone walking in the park the night before and found a football.

Part of me wanted to believe it was the same ball that had beaned me in the head. I smiled and nodded, occasionally glancing toward the kitchen door, where Sunlight and Cocoa Puff lay side-by-side, free of flour and drifting in and out of kitty cat dozes.

"We've got a lot to take care of this month," Gamma said. "The ghost tours. The cat hotel. Mr. Grote promised to recommend us now that he's won his cat show and the flour issue has been resolved."

"Thank goodness for that," Lauren put in.

"There's also the Tri-State Baking Competition next month. We'll have people coming from all over to stay in Gossip."

"Wait, why? We're hosting it?" I asked.

"The mayor applied last year, and we won the majority vote," Gamma said. "Palms were greased. So sayeth the grapevine. It's going to see a boom in tourism. A lot of new people to entertain and cook for."

"A lot of potential for chaos," I said.

"But of course. We would expect nothing less at the Gossip Inn, would we?" my grandmother asked.

"Ahem." The noise had come from the kitchen doorway, and all three of us turned.

Detective Goode, wearing a t-shirt and a pair of jeans, gave us a half-cocked smile. "Hi," he said. "Sorry to interrupt."

"As you should be," my grandmother said. "What is it you want, Detective? I believe you've done enough already."

"She means, congratulations on solving the case." I got up, brushing my hands off on my apron. "What do you need, Detective Goode?"

"Can I talk to you for a second, Miss Smith?"

"Do I have a choice?" I waved a hand. "Don't answer that. I'm coming." I followed him out into the hall, my grandmother's eyes tracking us both, narrowed to slits.

"Is Mrs. Franklin OK?" he asked.

Franklin was my grandmother's fake last name. "She's, uh, fine. Just having a rough morning."

Detective Goode walked all the way out onto the porch, into the rising heat of the morning, and sat down on the porch swing. I didn't join him. The porch swing reminded me of another time, another man, and another heartbreak.

"What do you want to talk to me about?" I asked.

"First off, when I'm not on the job, call me Aaron."

"Better to keep things professional," I said, slamming a barrier between us. "Is there a problem, Detective? Have you come to arrest me?"

"No. I wanted to thank you."

"Why?"

"Because I know you had a hand in what happened yesterday," he said.

I kept my mouth firmly shut.

"I can't prove it, of course, but I know that you did." He offered me another of his half-smiles, and my heart did a strange twiddly dance of betrayal. "Thanks for doing what you did. I'll admit I'm curious about how you pulled it off."

Still wasn't going to say anything.

"You don't give much away."

I shrugged. "I have no idea what you're talking about, Detective Goode. There's nothing to give away."

He rose from the porch swing and came closer, so close that he was mere inches from me, and the scent of his cologne nearly over-whelmed my senses. "Your hair looks nice, Charlotte," he whispered.

I stared up at him, wide-eyed. Words traveled through my mind, pinging and disappearing again.

Detective Goode reached up and brushed a strand of hair from my cheek. "Anyone ever told you, you've got a cute nose? Like a button." He pressed a finger to the end of my nose. "Be sure you keep it out of my cases from now on. Capeesh?"

I opened my mouth to snap at him, but he stunned me with a wink before tucking his hands into the pockets of his jeans and walking off.

My pulse hammered against the inside of my throat, and a slow blush spread up my neck and onto my face.

That man!

I spun to shout at him, but he was already too far down the pathway, and it would only make me look even more pathetic.

"I forbid it." My grandmother had appeared on the inn's threshold. "Charlotte, I forbid it. You are not to date that man."

"First," I said, raising a finger, my blush slowly receding, "as if you could stop me from doing anything." A lie. My grandmother could stop a moving train if she put her mind to it, I was sure of that. "And second, are you trying to make me throw up? That guy? Please. I've never met a more arrogant, a more assuming..."

Gamma gave me a knowing look. "He's one of those types."

"Which types?"

"The type who takes control of situations, who does what they shouldn't to get the right results, and who usually gets his way."

"You've just described us," I said. "We're like that."

"Exactly." My grandmother came over and slipped an arm around my shoulders. She squeezed me to her side, hugging me tightly. "That's why he's dangerous, Charlotte. He's too much like you."

I was so happy about the affection from my grandmother—she had never been the "touchy-feely" type—that I let the semi-insult slide. I hugged her in return.

"I'm proud of you, Charlie," she whispered, patting my back. "You've done yourself proud. You can truly call Gossip your home now."

The warmth of her words settled in my chest, expanding until I was sure I'd pop from contentment. She was right.

Gossip was my home. I finally had my place.

And I wouldn't let anyone threaten my town again.

Charlie and Gamma's adventures continue in the second book in The Gossip Cozy Mystery Series, The Case of the Key Lime Crimes, available from these retailers. Click to get it!

MORE FOR YOU...

Sign up to my mailing list and receive updates on future releases, as well as a **FREE** copy of *The Hawaiian Burger Murder* and *The Fully Loaded Burger Murder.*

They are two short cozy mysteries featuring characters from the Burger Bar Mystery series.

You can sign up by heading over to my Facebook page, or my website, rosiepointbooks@gmail.com, and hitting the "sign up" link!

ACKNOWLEDGMENTS

This book was a delight to write, but it wouldn't have been anywhere near as fun without the help and support of the people around me.

First, to my readers, my amazing "Curly Fries Lovers", and in particular to Lauren Dottin-Radel, Debi Paglia, Molly Hamblin, Dwayne Keller, Stephanie Walsh, Stephanie Keller, and Beverlee Smith for your continued support. You go above and beyond every time you read my books, and I'm not sure you even know how much that means to me.

A big thank you to Natasha White for her

advice regarding milling and logistics, for putting up with my strange questions, and for the invaluable emotional support.

And, of course, my dear family, my husband who endures my late night typing, constant book babble, and the occasional breakdown. And my son, who will forever be the reason I started writing in the first place.

Thank you.

Made in the USA
Monee, IL
24 February 2022